Heart in Hiding

**Center Point
Large Print**

**This Large Print Book carries the
Seal of Approval of N.A.V.H.**

Heart in Hiding

FRANCINE RIVERS

CENTER POINT PUBLISHING
THORNDIKE, MAINE

This Center Point Large Print edition
is published in the year 2006 by arrangement with
The Berkley Publishing Group, a division of
Penguin Group (USA) Inc.

Copyright © 1984 by Francine Rivers.

The text of this Large Print edition is unabridged. In other
aspects, this book may vary from the original edition. Printed in
Thailand. Set in 16-point Times New Roman type.

ISBN 1-58547-755-9

Library of Congress Cataloging-in-Publication Data

Rivers, Francine, 1947-
    Heart in hiding / Francine Rivers.--Center Point large print ed.
        p. cm.
    ISBN 1-58547-755-9 (lib. bdg. : alk. paper)
    1. Large type books. 2. Religious fiction. I. Title.

PS3568.I83165H43 2006
813'.54--dc22
                                                    2005031249

8/07

Heart in Hiding

1

HEARING THE CRUNCH of gravel in her driveway, Annie Seaton tossed a sprig of geranium into her old tin bucket and straightened. She quickly wiped her hands on her apron and tucked damp tendrils of wheat-blond hair back from her sun- and work-warmed face.

Money was short this month and a guest at Makawsa wouldn't just be welcome; it would be a godsend. Katie had a dental checkup on Friday, and Dr. McDowell required payment on the day of the appointment. The bill for the cord of oak dumped down near the carport was overdue, and the garage had requested cash before ordering parts for her '72 Ford Pinto.

September was always slow, what with children back in school. Late October usually picked up with the beginning of the salmon run, but Annie couldn't wait that long. Money had been squeaky tight before, but not to the point where every penny screamed. She had been lying awake nights recently worrying about finances.

If only Brent sent child support . . .

She stopped herself. No "if onlys," she reminded herself firmly. She would manage somehow. Hadn't she up till now?

While waiting to see who was coming up her

driveway, Annie said a fervent prayer and crossed her fingers for good measure.

A dusty blue van with a bug-splattered windshield and a dent on the right front side rattled up the last section of her road and pulled to a stop in front of the house.

Annie sighed heavily. Whoever was driving that van was well enough equipped for camping that he wouldn't be looking for a room to rent. Frowning slightly, she wondered why he had pulled in at all. Surely, if he needed directions, he could have asked in Gualala, just down the road a few miles. Or could this be someone she knew?

A man emerged. Even at that distance she knew she had never seen him before. She would have remembered.

He was very tall and broad-shouldered, with a thick mane of dark brown hair and a full beard. There was something compelling about him in spite of the green fatigue jacket, on the right sleeve of which had been sewn a small American flag, and the well-worn, blue-white jeans that fit him like a denim skin.

He stood by the steps looking up at her 1924 farmhouse, which she had painted glorious Swedish barn red with white trim. The window boxes overflowed with red, pink, and purple petunias, white sweet alyssum, and golden calendulas. He raked his hands through his too-long hair, which brushed well below his collar, and she guessed he was making an attempt to tidy himself. As he went up the front steps, she saw he was wearing heavy hiking boots.

He looked like a modern-day prospector or one of the army of bohemians who camped along the Pacific coast during good weather months. His rough yet commanding appearance made her think seriously about taking four steps backward and disappearing into the thicket of yellow Canary Island broom at the edge of her flower garden.

The stranger pulled the brass ring on the front door. Annie heard the faint bell peal clearly across the lawn and gravel driveway. She should call out to him, yet she hesitated, uncertain. Even if he was looking for a place to stay, which she doubted, she wasn't sure she wanted this man under her roof.

She had long since gotten over her inner-city habit of locking and deadbolting doors, but this time she wished she had locked it. This unexpected visitor looked perfectly capable of walking right on in and helping himself to the stainless steel flatware, and she certainly wasn't brave enough to stop him!

But he didn't.

He waited, rang again, waited a little longer, then turned to walk slowly along her porch. Stopping at the end, he looked out toward her vegetable garden, which was surrounded by wire-mesh fencing to keep out the deer. A ground squirrel had burrowed underneath and was in the process of stealing another ripe tomato. Gopher mounds abounded because she didn't have the heart to drown, poison, or shoot them, as was prescribed by the locals.

"It was gophers run the Roosians out of Fort Ross. Nothing else," one old timer had told her. "Thousands of the little bastards. You gotta kill 'em, or they'll take over!"

But her garden produced more than enough for everyone, including rodents. And vagrants . . .

Studying the man, Annie wondered if he was just hungry and looking for a handout. He was lean and hard without an extra ounce of flesh—at least what she could see of him was. Of course, beneath that heavy army jacket he could be hiding a beer belly. Nevertheless, he wouldn't be the first rough looking, pocket-empty young traveler to stop off. A sack of tomatoes, zucchini, bell peppers, and Jerusalem artichokes would send him on his way amiably enough.

She started forward, but saw he had lost interest in her vegetables and was now contemplating her dilapidated barn. It needed a new roof on the front side, but what money she had saved last year had gone into fixing up the section that housed her power tools and into two truck loads of gravel for her badly rutted driveway. Besides, the barn provided "atmosphere." Since coming to Makawsa six years ago, she'd sold a hundred or more watercolors of it.

The man had spotted Mabel, her milk cow and "udder failure," and Hortense, the bad-tempered billy goat, both grazing down the hill.

A loud noise startled the stranger. Annie almost laughed aloud. It was just past ten A.M., and Prince Charming, the rooster, had finally managed to make his perch, while Snow White and the Seven Dwarfs, the bantam hens, pecked indifferently below. Another long night, she thought with amusement before returning her full attention to the stranger.

His gaze had reached the flower garden, with its swirls and mounds of colors—brilliant orange-gold California poppies, baskets-of-gold, red geraniums, yellow calendulas, blue cornflowers and marguerites, pink bachelor's buttons, purple alyssum, white daisies, and *her*. . . .

The stranger seemed to freeze, staring at her across a distance of some two hundred feet. She watched him grip her railing.

Lifting her chin, she called, "Hello! What can I do for you, sir?"

She picked up her heavy metal bucket just in case he proved threatening up close.

"Hello," he called back.

She couldn't tell much from his voice, which was as deep and rough as he was. He let go of the railing and walked along the porch, still staring across at her. Men who stared at her always made her feel uncomfortable.

He came down the steps and walked toward her. She noticed his loose-limbed, purely masculine swagger. Some men tried hard to emulate that kind of walk and failed dismally. This man must come by it naturally—an unconscious revelation of power and virility.

He stopped a few feet away from her, and she

looked up into glowing, intense blue eyes. Her heart thumped hard. He smiled. She felt a warm shiver travel through her body, spiraling in the part of her that, for the past seven years, she had tried to deny even existed. She had seen that kind of male smile before, but it had never made her heart hammer in this wild, flash-dance rhythm.

"Are you lost?" she asked, embarrassed when her voice cracked.

"I was," he admitted in a deep, easy voice that matched his walk and was like a seductive touch on her tense nerves. "But I'm not any longer."

She immediately sensed trouble.

He was taking in every aspect of her face—her wide hazel eyes, the arch of her brows, her straight nose, her high cheekbones, the square line of her jaw, her stubborn chin, and her mouth. Especially her mouth. She could *feel* him looking at her mouth.

Suddenly she felt as if she were sitting before a blazing fire in the middle of a hot August afternoon.

"You look exactly like someone out of a Victorian picture," he told her. "My grandmother had one in her parlor. I think it was called *Girl Carrying Water Bucket.* All you lack is the white bandanna covering your hair."

The oversight didn't seem to bother him as his gaze swept down her faded ankle-length dress and soiled white apron then back up to the sweat-dampened curls framing her face. His gaze moved down again along

14

the length of the thick braid and paused on her full breasts.

She could feel her face heating up. "Were you looking for Makawsa?" she asked.

"Not exactly. I pulled in on impulse. Did you paint that sign?"

"Yes," she answered. Her tole-painted morning glories surrounding the calligraphied MAKAWSA—ROOM FOR RENT—WEEKENDS ONLY had drawn many compliments in the past. One antique dealer from Healdsburg had paid her a whopping two hundred dollars to do a folk art sign for his store.

The stranger shrugged out of his fatigue jacket and slung it casually over one hard-muscled shoulder. He put his free hand into a jeans pocket. His stance was indolent, relaxed. He had no beer belly, she noticed. The fitted western shirt hugged a decidedly broad chest and was tucked into the narrow waist of his jeans.

He was too potently male. Or was she simply too aware of him? His disturbingly warm eyes worried her. The message in them was all too clear.

"It's a little warm up here," he remarked innocuously.

"Yes. We're in the Banana Belt, just out of the prevailing winds from the ocean," she explained. But words died quickly between them. He just seemed to want to drink the sight of her in, and she couldn't keep from looking him over either.

How long had it been since she'd felt this stir of

attraction? Yet *stir* wasn't a strong enough description. How could she be standing here looking at this stranger and thinking of the man-woman thing? She nervously fingered her pewter cross.

"I know I look a mess, but I'm safe enough," he told her, noticing and, to her relief, misunderstanding her agitation. "I've been camping up in the Trinity Alps for the past week, and I haven't had a chance to clean up."

At least his beard was trimmed. He reminded her of a cigarette ad on a billboard showing a macho male in a red and black wool shirt and spiked boots. *A hunk.*

She supposed he was trying to make her relax, but the sexy purr in his voice sent her senses reeling. She wished strongly that he would just decide she was dim-witted and leave. She couldn't remember ever being so physically attracted to a man. Even the first time she had seen Brent her blood hadn't gone all warm like this.

"There's no need to be frightened of me," the stranger said.

"I'm not."

"You don't sound convincing." He came closer and held out his big, square hand. "I'm Matt Hagen." Her heart turned a somersault and stuck high in her throat.

Automatically she brushed off her hand and held it out. His fingers closed firmly around hers, swallowing them in hard warmth. Feathery sensations traveled up her arm, spread across her breasts, and sank slowly lower and lower.

"And yours?" he asked with raised eyebrows.

"Annie," she stammered. "Annie Seaton."

"Well, Annie, contrary to looks, I'm not a marijuana grower taking a sojourn in the California redwoods," he teased. "I'm perfectly harmless."

She knew that was the first outright lie he uttered. This man was anything but harmless.

With a gentle tug she freed her fingers from his and gripped the handle of her bucket with both hands. "Well, Mr. Hagen, I'm afraid I don't have facilities open to the public. There's a campground down the highway a piece where you can get a shower and a shave."

His eyes lit up in amusement. "It would be quicker and easier if I rented your room."

Her heart stopped. Contrary to what she had been praying for when he drove up, this was exactly what she didn't want to hear from him. She was desperate for a boarder, but another look into his mesmerizing, seductive blue eyes told her clearly that she didn't need this particular man sleeping under her roof. She shook her head.

"Never judge a man by the van he drives or the length of his beard. My credit's good."

She was thankful he had given her a good reason to turn him down. "I don't accept credit of any kind."

"That's all right. I'll pay cash. How much do you want for the weekend?" He reached into his back pocket and brought out a worn, brown leather wallet. It looked pathetically thin.

"I . . . I'm sorry," she said, embarrassed and grasping for something convincing to say to make him go away. "I'm holding the room for someone else." It was a lie, and she hoped he couldn't tell that just by looking into her eyes. Her face felt too warm, but she met his penetrating gaze as stoically as she could.

"Just careful, Annie?"

She bristled at the way he said her name. She had hardly met the man, yet he said her name as though they meant something to each other. That kind of too-quick charm and familiarity had always annoyed her. She resented how she felt when he looked at her, but, most of all, she resented Matt Hagen's very presence and the reawakening sense of female vulnerability and physical desire she thought she had long since buried.

"*Mrs.* Seaton," she told him coldly enough to freeze mercury. She was sure that would quickly kill his potent charm.

But rather than being nonplussed or reduced to silence, he looked pointedly at her ringless hands, which were still clutching the bucket handle. "Divorced or widowed?"

"Good day, Mr. Hagen."

"My apologies," he said ruefully. "I'm glad you're cautious with strangers, Annie. A woman on her own should be." He turned and walked back toward his van.

She watched him go with a faint frown. Why should she feel so guilty about turning him away? *He* didn't look upset. What was this dangerous, illogical impulse to call out and ask him to stay?

It would be a big mistake, she knew. She was all too aware of the sexual aura radiating from him. Men as attractive as Matt Hagen were fully aware of their appeal. They *used* it. Perhaps he even lived on it by using it to get women to give him a room and meals on credit. It had happened to other people. It was easy enough to wave an empty wallet and pretend you had the money while flashing a provocative smile that made a woman aware she was a woman. If Annie had held her tongue, he'd probably have opened up his wallet and said something like, "Oh, I'll have to write you a check. I used my last dollar paying a bridge toll." And by the end of the weekend he'd be selling her the whole bridge.

As Matt turned the van around, she saw him raise his hand out the window in a final salute. Vague disappointment stirred in her as she watched him leave.

She knew she was overly cynical where men were concerned, but she wouldn't apologize for it. Better safe than sorry, as the saying went. Annie knew all she ever wanted to know about the devastating effect on a woman's emotions caused by a charismatic man.

2

"SUZANNE'S MOM AND dad are taking her to San Francisco again on Saturday," Katie informed Annie while munching on a still-warm oatmeal cookie. Annie's heart plunged, knowing what was coming next. "She's going to get to go to the aquarium," Katie went on glumly. "They're even going to stay in a big hotel. Couldn't we do that, too, Mommy? Please?"

How Annie wished she could say yes. But no matter how hard she worked, she just couldn't seem to make more than what was necessary to pay the mortgage, taxes, and bills and save a little for Katie's college fund. She wouldn't promise her daughter anything she couldn't give.

"I wish we could, honey," Annie told her softly, pausing in the middle of drying the washed cookie sheet to kiss her cheek. Her throat tightened as she saw disappointment dim the sparkle in Katie's wide blue eyes. Eyes like Brent's. It was the only thing she had inherited from her father.

Katie's lower lip protruded, quivering. "How come everybody else gets to do it, but we *never* can?"

It was a childish exaggeration, but it hurt Annie terribly because it was partly true. Suzanne, Katie's best friend, went some place special at least once a month.

"We just don't have enough money, Katie," Annie answered honestly.

"We would if we moved down to Santa Rosa and you got a *real* job," Katie pleaded.

"I do have a real job." As it was, she worked far more than an eight-hour day, but Katie couldn't understand that. Annie worked most when Katie was at school or in bed asleep. Often she was in her workroom far past midnight, completing orders for the coastal gift shops of mini-wreaths, ink sketches of tourist attractions such as Fort Ross, and small wildflower watercolors she matted ready for framing. And there was her tole painting, the folk art flowers and designs so popular in Scandinavian homes and gaining appeal in the States. Annie had painted the kissing birds and flower designs on her kitchen cabinets.

"We've talked it over before, Katie," Annie said. "If I worked a nine-to-five job, you'd have to stay with a sitter all the time. Here I can do the crafts for gift shops and earn a little extra money when we have guests. We can be together."

"I want to go to the aquarium," Katie persisted, her eyes filling with tears. "If we moved into town, we could go, couldn't we? We could be together on Saturdays and Sundays, and I wouldn't mind being with a sitter if she was nice 'cause we'd go to special places every weekend. Please?"

Annie's heart ached. She felt selfish and mean for wanting to raise her seven-year-old daughter in a cozy

21

old farmhouse rather than in a suburban cracker box. True, the four acres of Makawsa weren't a big city park with swings and slides and elaborate jungle gyms, but she and Katie had redwoods up on the hills and the apple tree with the tire swing. And the Gualala River ran past, not more than a few hundred yards from their front door, on its way to the sea.

How many other children could watch deer graze in their front yard at dusk or see salmon run in late October or early November? Here they could have a milk cow and a flock of chickens, and a billy goat and their own vegetable garden. Here they could breath fresh, ocean-scented air and know all the people in town by their first names.

But none of that helped to convince a lonely little girl that Makawsa was the best place to live.

"Katie, if we moved to town, the best I could do would be to work as a secretary in an office. We couldn't live in a house. All we could afford would be a tiny condominium with a balcony hardly big enough for some potted plants." She tipped up Katie's chin and watched two huge tears roll down her smooth, flushed cheeks. "I would give you the moon if I could, honey, but this is the best I can do."

It was the closest thing to paradise that she herself had found in her life.

Katie sniffed and reached out to hug her mother. Annie rested her cheek on her daughter's head, squeezing her eyes tightly closed, swallowing back her own tears.

"Would you settle for a beach cookout instead of the aquarium?" Annie offered, forcing a smile and lifting her daughter's chin. "We could barbecue hamburgers on the hibachi and corn-on-the-cob in tinfoil, and build sand castles, and look for hermit crabs and starfish in the tidepools. We could stay until the sunset warms the water."

Katie's brimming eyes brightened and her lip stopped trembling. "Marshmallows, too?" she wheedled.

Annie laughed. "And marshmallows," she conceded. "I think there's a bag left from our last cookout. Why don't you check the pantry?"

"Super!" Katie cried, jumping down from the high kitchen stool. "Can we go right now?"

"As soon as I get these trays dried and can put the hamburger patties together. You find the marshmallows and see about charcoal in the carport. The hibachi is still in the car."

Katie had already produced the bag of marshmallows and was catapulting out the kitchen door. Annie smiled as she heard the screen door bang shut. But within seconds it creaked open again. She frowned. "Katie?" She couldn't have gone to the carport that fast. Katie came in and slumped on the stool. "Someone's coming up the driveway," she said glumly, her eyes brimming with tears again. "Couldn't we not answer, Mommy? Just this once? Couldn't we go to the beach instead. *Please?*"

Annie took off her apron and hugged her daughter.

"I know you're disappointed, honey. We'll still go on our cookout. We'll just have to postpone it for a few minutes." At the look on Katie's face, Annie almost hoped it wasn't a guest coming.

She stepped into her moccasins by the front door and went out to see who had arrived. A blue van was parked in front of the house.

Her heart jumped as though someone had poked her with a cattle prod. It just couldn't be the same one, she thought frantically. Surely Matt Hagen wouldn't come back. Besides, this van was bright blue, washed and waxed. But there was that dent on the right front side. She walked over to the railing and watched him slide out of the van.

It wasn't just the van that looked different. Gone were the fatigue jacket, faded jeans, and dirty hiking boots. Gone was the dark beard. His hair was still long, but soft and shiny from a recent shampoo and brushing. He was now wearing tailored tan slacks, a white polo shirt, and an expensive brown leather sports jacket. He put his foot on her bottom step, and she looked down to see that he was even wearing polished brown brogues.

"I hope I'm a little more presentable this time around," he said, winking up at her. Her heart pounded faster with each step he took, until it was racing wildly as he reached eye level, two steps below her. He was heart-stoppingly handsome.

Opening his jacket, he produced a single long-stemmed yellow rose around which was tied a thin red satin ribbon. "For you," he said softly. "I didn't see any roses in your garden."

Her hand trembled slightly as she accepted it. "I've never had much luck with them. Mildew."

He grinned. "Mildew will get you every time."

She blushed, feeling foolish.

"Have you rented that room yet?"

Katie came out the front door and saved Annie from having to answer. "Oh, super! You've got a camper just like the ones down at the beach in summer. Can I see inside?"

"Katie," Annie said in a quiet reprimand.

Matt laughed. "Sure, why not?" He took out his keys and handed them over.

"No, I don't think so . . . Katie, I said no," Annie said, seeing her daughter already skipping down the steps. Katie halted. "Give the keys back to Mr. Hagen, please."

Katie didn't look pleased, but she obeyed.

"Sorry, Kitten," Matt said, taking the keys and pocketing them. Katie sat down on the steps and gave her mother an accusing, hurt look. Matt's gaze went to Annie. "Have your other guests shown up?"

Again Katie interceded. "Oh, we aren't expecting anyone tonight," she volunteered. "No one's coming for sure until the salmon run, and that's weeks away." Annie tried to silence her with a look, but Katie had eyes only for the big, handsome man who owned the van. "Mom's been just dying for someone to come so she can pay the dentist."

25

At that precise moment Annie would gladly have sunk into the ground. Her face was on fire, and she was aware of the faint smile tugging at Matt Hagen's sensual mouth. "The dentist, hmm?" he said commiserately. "I'd think you'd want to barricade the driveway rather than have company."

Katie grinned broadly in agreement.

"How much does your mom charge for a room?"

"I don't know," Katie admitted with a shrug. "But it's not enough 'cause there's never anything left over for us to go to the aquarium."

"Kathleen Patricia Seaton," Annie said, mortified. Nothing like spilling all the family beans at once!

Matt laughed, a pleasing, deep unrestrained sound that rippled warmly along Annie's taut body. He bent at the waist and extended his hand. "My name's Matt. And who're you, Kitten?"

"Katie. But I like 'Kitten' better." She put her small, tanned hand into his big one and gazed raptly up at him. Annie wondered distractedly whether he had the same effect on little girls that he did on big ones.

Matt straightened and glanced at Annie. His mouth curved. Her heart raced. "How about it, Mrs. Seaton. May I rent your room?"

She worried her lower lip, trying to think of a plausible excuse to turn him away again. She gauged him carefully. He looked straight into her eyes with alarming implacability and warmth. The sinking sensation in her stomach offset the soaring one in her chest.

"The room is sixty-five dollars a night," she told him, boosting the price and hoping it would be enough of a shock to make him change his mind about staying.

"Fair enough," he said without hesitation, stunning her. "Is that with meals, or do they cost extra?"

The glint in his blue eyes was unnerving. She was sure he knew she had raised the price to discourage him. But how, unless the truth was written clearly on her face or he had read her small advertisement in *Sunset* magazine.

"With meals. Payment in advance," she added more clearly.

He withdrew the same worn wallet. At least that much hadn't changed. It still looked pathetically thin, and she felt almost guilty as he extracted some money and handed it to her. "That should cover a couple days."

"Thank you," she said flatly, trapped now. His fingers lightly brushed hers as she accepted the payment, and her whole sensory system seemed to go into overload. She could smell the faint, tangy aftershave he wore. She looked up into his eyes and was appalled at the erotic image that flashed into her mind.

His pupils dilated until she could see her own reflection in them, like a picture imprinting itself on his brain. "All settled now?" he asked softly.

She blinked. "Pardon me?"

"The room. It's mine?"

She let out her breath on a startled sigh. "Yes, of

course." How long had she been standing here like an idiot just staring up at him? "If you'll get your things, I'll show you the way."

"Be right with you." He went down the steps. "How about some assistance, Kitten?"

"Okay!" Katie jumped up and, before Annie could protest again, almost dived into the back of the van as soon as Matt opened it. She was still inside when he lifted out a big green, ancient-looking duffel bag.

"Mommy! Matt's got a CB radio just like in *Smokey and the Bandit*!"

Annie noticed the size of the duffel bag and wondered whether everything he owned was in it. Just how long did Matt Hagen expect to stay? She glanced down at the bills she had forgotten to count. Enough for *three* days. Well, Monday morning, bright and early, she would see him to the door in a friendly fashion, and thank God when he hit the road again.

"Don't you think my daughter should come out of your van before she breaks something?"

"She can't break anything that I haven't broken a couple of times myself already. Let her have a good look. You worry too much, Annie."

There was that familiar tone again. Moments later he was even opening the front door of *her* house as calmly as though he belonged here. She preceded him into the foyer and, before she could stop herself, stepped out of her shoes again. He chuckled softly from behind her. "So that's why you were barefoot in the garden."

28

She stepped hastily back into them wondering what it was about this man that seemed to render her half-witted. "You're free to use the living room," she told him, gesturing, but hardly giving him a chance to look around before she started down the hallway off to the right. "This way, please." She passed her room, and the bathroom on the left, her workroom on the right, Katie's room on the left, another spare bedroom on the right, and opened the door at the end of the hall to the master bedroom she rented out. "This is it," she said, stepping inside. "I think you'll find it comfortable."

"I'm used to a van, so anything bigger will seem like a palace."

She walked across to open the window, more to put distance between them than to let fresh air into the already freshened room. A breeze gently rippled the sheer white curtains as she turned around. "There's a luggage stand in the closet and an extra blanket, should you need it. It gets cold up here at night."

"Does it?" There was a teasing glint in his eyes.

She looked away. "You have a private bath, of course."

"And a real canopy bed. This is going to be a first for me," he said, and she heard the amusement in his tone.

"Honeymooners have liked it," she said without thinking.

He laughed softly. "It does lend romance." He stepped closer to the bed and swung his duffel bag up on it. The rugged soldier's carrier looked out of place against the quilted spread. Masculinity invading femininity. The contrast was even stronger when he put his tanned hand on the quilt and pressed down. "Nice and hard, just the way I like it."

Something about the way Matt Hagen ran his hand along the spread and then raised it to lightly ruffle the net canopy she had macraméd made her absolutely sure that he was a man who wouldn't be satisfied with ten minutes of making love.

"You like things nice and old-fashioned, don't you?" he asked. His slow, sensual smile made her fingers curl into her palms.

She wasn't sure whether he was referring to the decor she had chosen for the room or making an observation about her. She wished she had changed into blue jeans and a blouse rather than remaining in her long skirt and putting on a fresh apron.

"Ultramodern would hardly be appropriate on a country farm, don't you think?" she said.

"I wasn't criticizing, Annie." He studied her with a quizzical frown. "Why so defensive with me?"

She knew exactly why, of course, but she could hardly blurt out that she found him distressingly attractive, that he made her heart race and her breath catch and her imagination run riot. He made her aware that she was a woman, and that she hadn't been touched or kissed or made love to by a man in more than seven years.

"Dinner is served at six," she said. "You can have whatever you want."

"Anything?"

He was teasing her, but she was annoyed at her response and his lightness in the face of it. "Beef, lamb, pork, chicken, or fish," she told him coolly.

"I'll take hamburger, corn-on-the-cob, and marsh-mallows. What time are we all leaving for the beach?"

Her mouth fell open.

"We *are* going on a cookout this evening, aren't we?" he asked. "Or did I get my information wrong?"

Katie had certainly wasted no time. Annie was going to have to have a talk with that child!

"No, I don't think so. I'll take Katie another time."

"Why not tonight? It seems to matter to her." His expression was serious.

"She'll get over it."

He rested his hand on the bedpost as she moved restlessly away from the window to the desk in the corner, nervously checking to see whether she had left out the hand-pressed flower stationery she'd made.

"Why should she have to get over it?" he asked. "What's your objection to going ahead with your plans for the evening?"

She looked at him, trying not to stare at the broad expanse of chest revealed by the snug-fitting pullover beneath his open sports jacket. "Because what I cook on a beach isn't what I serve to my guests here at Makawsa. If it were, no one would ever come back."

He crossed his arms and leaned indolently against the bedpost. "Not edible?"

"Edible, yes, but not fare for someone paying sixty-five dollars a night for room and board. I'd think you would want chateaubriand."

"I won't complain. I promise."

She didn't want him to come. The beach was something special, something private.

"I have some nice fat salmon steaks," she offered, hoping to entice him. He shook his head. She sighed. "Beach fare is very *simple.*"

"Simplicity is best. I'm a meat-and-potatoes man, or rather, a hamburger-and-a-bun man." He winked.

"You don't understand." She stopped herself from explaining the emotions involved and plunged into practicalities instead. "I'm not the world's greatest barbecue chef, Mr. Hagen. I do much better over a gas stove."

"Well, I do all right, so I'll barbecue the hamburgers," he told her. "Problem solved."

Angry now, she stuffed his yellow rose into a vase already containing yellow Canary Island broom that she had arranged on the antique dresser she had bought at a garage sale and refinished. She walked briskly to the door. "Fine. But I suggest you change back into your *usual* clothes. They are far more suitable attire for the beach."

"Yes, ma'am."

She stormed downstairs to the kitchen and began gathering the rest of what they would need for the picnic. She had mixed more than enough ground beef and seasonings, since she always made enough patties to freeze some for a later cookout. She stacked things carefully in the big wicker basket, then bent to pull a big onion from the old-fashioned dry bin. She cut off the skin and began slicing it. Halfway through, she belatedly remembered the wad of bills she had put in her skirt pocket.

She stretched to reach into a high cabinet and just managed to grasp the empty coffee can in which she hid her money until she could take it to the bank. She was prying off the plastic lid when the kitchen door swung open, hitting her in the backside and making her stumble forward. The can flew out of her hand and clanged across the room, rolling underneath the stool.

"Good Lord, I'm sorry," Matt apologized. "Are you all right?"

"Yes," she gasped, embarrassed.

He glanced from the can, which had rolled out from under the stool and come to rest in the corner, to the money in her fist.

She looked at his faded blue safari shirt, hand-tooled leather belt with a brass buckle, and thigh-snug, pale jeans. He was wearing his boots again. Some men could look devastating in anything. Or nothing.

Now, why had she allowed herself to think that?

Matt crossed the room, bent, and retrieved the can. She watched the muscles work beneath the thin cotton shirt as he squatted down and straightened again. "You weren't planning on putting that money in this can, were you?"

"What about it?" she asked defensively, taking the can from him and stuffing the wad of bills inside.

33

"A coffee can is about as obvious as a cookie jar, Annie."

She stepped past him and stretched up on her tiptoes to slide the can back into its hiding place. "It's so obvious, no one would think of it. Besides, I'll be taking it to the bank on Monday, just as soon as you leave."

He laughed, gazing down at her. "Trying to make me feel welcome?"

Her face burned.

His smile became rueful, his expression curious and assessing. She stepped around him trying to escape his profound attention. Picking up the knife, she resumed slicing the onion. He took the knife from her hand. "I think it's safer all the way around if I handle this," he told her with an amused grin.

"I'm not the violent type, Mr. Hagen."

"No, but you could hurt yourself. You're shaking."

She turned away to tuck napkins and a bottle of ketchup into the basket, trying to ignore his masculine presence in her kitchen. It was impossible. Even when she wasn't looking at him, she was intensely aware of him, as though every cell in her body was a homing device centered on him.

"Got a container for these?" he asked, nodding toward the onion slices as he rinsed the knife under the faucet.

"Under the counter. I'll get it." She produced a neat Tupperware container with a white plastic lid.

"Pretty organized. My mother always spent half an

hour trying to match containers to lids." He shuffled the onion slices, tapped them together, and dropped them into the container, which snapped shut with a press of his forefinger.

She took the container from him, plunked it into the basket, and closed the rattan flaps. "All set. I just have to change, and then we can leave." She started to lift the basket.

"I'll handle this," he murmured close to her ear, and she felt his hand slide around her waist, spreading across her stomach as he drew her back, his other hand taking the basket from her grip. For just a moment she felt the hard length of his body against her back. She stepped quickly away, shaken. "You and Katie will need some jackets for later," he said, holding the kitchen door open for her.

In her room she debated whether or not to wear shorts and then decided on brown stovepipe pants. She pulled on a lightweight green sweater and got her parka and Katie's before going outside. This time she locked the front door.

Katie was talking volubly to Matt, who was leaning against his van listening attentively. They both glanced up as Annie came down the steps. "Did you remember to get the charcoal, Katie?"

"It's in the van," Matt answered.

"Matt's going to drive us in his van, Mommy," Katie informed her, her eyes bright.

"And whose idea was that, young lady?"

"Please. I want to ride in the van and Matt said—"

"I think we'll take our car," she told him, not wanting to get into that blue van.

"Why?" he asked, straightening.

Who knew what had gone on inside it? It would be like sitting in a man's bedroom, locked in a seat belt so she couldn't get out. But that was hardly a *logical* reason; it made no real sense. "I know where we're going. You don't," she told him instead.

"Give me directions." He opened the van door for her. Katie scrambled into the back.

"Katie!" She gave him a pointed look. "Mr. Hagen, I really think—"

"It'll take less time than arguing, don't you think?" he interrupted, gesturing for her to get in.

"I've got my seat belt on already, Mommy!" Katie called, and Annie was well aware what it would probably take to get her out now. Grimly, she slid into the front seat. Matt closed the door, making sure it was locked. She watched him walk around the front and get in on the other side. The gearshift lever separated them.

He put the key into the ignition and started the van. Glancing up into his rearview mirror, he winked at Katie. Annie heard her daughter giggling smugly. He worked the gear twice before getting it into reverse. "Needs a little work," he told her, turning slightly.

His hand brushed her shoulder as he rested it on the back of her seat while turning the van around. She watched his strong brown hand grasp the gearshift lever to shove it forward into position. She closed her eyes as a heavy, pulsing excitement filled her.

Gravel crunched loudly beneath the rolling wheels of the van. He turned left, heading west for the ocean. Two miles down the road, he let the van idle at the Highway 1 intersection. "Which way?"

"Left," Katie answered from the back.

Annie put out her hand. "Oh, no! I forgot the hibachi. It's in the back of my car."

"Never mind. I've got what we need." He pulled out onto the two-lane highway and headed south.

"I forgot the blanket, too."

"Just relax. You're beginning to make me nervous." Matt laughed softly. His face was filled with confidence.

Annie glanced back to make sure Katie wasn't into something. She was buried in a magazine, and Annie caught her breath. She let it out again with relief when she saw it was a *National Geographic* and not a *Playboy.* The issue was on space, not naked aborigines. She turned around again and caught Matt grinning at her. "What were you expecting?" he asked.

She laughed at herself. "A mother can't be too careful, and you *are a* single male."

They drove in silence for several miles. "That's it just over there," she told him, pointing.

"You mean that little wide spot in the road?"

"There's a goat trail down to the beach," Annie explained. She suddenly had an idea of how to avoid taking him to their special place. "Salt Point is much better. It's farther down the coast, but there are picnic facilities there and—"

"Awww, Mommy," Katie protested with immediate vehemence. "Salt Point is *boring*." She leaned forward. "This is much better, Matt. No one ever comes here. It's all ours, and there are tide pools and sea gulls and shells and things. You just have to be careful going down."

Matt pulled off the road. Annie sighed inwardly. Katie was all too eager to share their private paradise. She was out of her seat belt ready to jump out of the van door as soon as Matt pulled to a stop. "Slow down, young lady. You're going to wait for us," Annie told her.

"Ah, gee." Katie groaned. "Can't you make it down on your own?"

Annie's mouth twitched. "Well, I don't know. Considering my advanced years, I may need some help."

"Matt can help you. He's older than you are, but he can make it."

Matt laughed. "I'll keep an eye on her. I'll go first, so if she falls, she'll land on me." His eyes glinted merrily at her rigid face.

Annie carried the basket. Matt shouldered the bag of charcoal and carried a grate and a sleeping bag.

Katie beat them both to the beach, kicking off her tennis shoes and running for the water as soon as she reached the bottom of the narrow, winding trail down the steep hillside. As always, the small cove was deserted.

"Don't forget to watch for sneakers, Katie!" Annie called out.

Matt glanced at her. "Sneakers?"

"Unexpected waves," she explained, barely meeting his eyes. She couldn't move farther down the trail until he did. And he wasn't. "The calmer the day looks, the more danger there can be," she added. "A lot of people have been washed off the rocks because they turned their backs to the sea."

"It's not just the sea that sneaks up on you and knocks you off your feet." The warmth and the open message in his eyes held her transfixed. "You know, Annie, I can't remember the last time I saw a woman blush."

"Would you please keep moving, or shall I go first?"

"It might prove a little difficult trying to get around me. We're on a narrow trail going one way, Annie."

Her heart beat heavily as she looked into his eyes. He returned her gaze steadily, then turned slowly away to begin moving down the trail again.

The water sparkled with incandescent, shifting light from the sun's rays. Waves topped with greenish foam rolled onto the sandy beach; the water turned deep blue farther out. The air carried a tang of salt.

Annie set down the heavy basket and straightened, avoiding Matt's eyes and watching Katie. Like a sandpiper, the small distant figure of her pigtailed child darted back and forth with the ebb and flow of the ocean. But instead of pecking for sand crabs, like the sandpipers, Katie paused to pick up broken seashells and pretty colored rocks before running again to outdistance the onrushing waves.

"Does she ever stop moving?" Matt asked.

Annie smiled. "She never walks. She always skips or runs."

"I'll bet you were the same way when you were her age."

She glanced back at him. He had set his things down, and his hands were free. He came close and slowly ran a tormenting finger down the length of her thick braid, which lay across her left shoulder against her breast. Her breath caught. She should protest his personal touch.

"And you still wear pigtails," he murmured softly, his eyes teasing.

She drew back. Other guests had made passes at her, but she'd never responded to any of them. Turning them down and putting things on the right plane had always been easy before.

She shook her head, looking warily up at him. "I'd better get things set up."

"No hurry, is there?"

"It'll take a while to get the charcoal burning properly."

"I'll take care of that."

"You don't have to do it."

"Annie, it's a man's job to get the fire going."

Hers was already burning hotter than she wanted, and

40

it would roast her own goose if she didn't take care.

He laughed softly. "Don't look so skeptical. I know what I'm doing."

She was sure he did, and she wasn't thinking about lighting charcoal. Forcing herself to look away, she sought sight of Katie in the distance.

"Why don't you go on down so you can keep a closer eye on her? I'll take care of things up here and follow in a few minutes."

Deciding not to argue, Annie left him to it. She kicked off her moccasins and headed down the beach toward Katie, glad to get away from Matt Hagen.

3

LOOKING BACK UP the beach, Annie saw Matt standing near the smoking charcoal fire. His head was back, the sea air ruffling his thick dark hair, his legs splayed as though bracing himself, his thumbs hooked into his front belt-loops. He looked a natural part of things— relaxed, carefree, disturbingly attractive. She couldn't imagine him behind a desk in a big city.

He glanced toward her, and she lowered her head quickly to look at the sand as she walked along the waterline, the white foam licking chillingly around her ankles. She had rolled up her brown pants to keep them from getting wet.

She supposed she did look old-fashioned. Or perhaps out-of-sync with everyone else would be a better way of putting it. Her mother once said she should have been part of the Katharine Hepburn generation. While everyone else was wearing jeans that looked spray-painted on, she stuck to her baggy pants.

Matt was still watching her. She felt nervous beneath such interested scrutiny. Then he was walking down the beach toward her. Her heart began to thud. She told herself again that he would be leaving Makawsa on Monday morning.

He came close. His smile made her stomach tighten and her knees weaken. "May I walk with you?"

"I don't own the beach," she said, softening her words with a smile.

"Why do I have the feeling I'm intruding on your private space?" he asked seriously.

She looked away self-consciously.

"You've never brought anyone down to this beach before, have you? It's been yours and Katie's," he said when she didn't answer. "Look, I'm sorry, Annie. I . . . hell," he murmured, rubbing the back of his neck. They walked for a few yards without speaking. "It *is* magical here," he told her. "I can understand why you'd want to keep it to yourself."

Wishing her heart would stop pounding so hard, she pushed her hands into her front pockets and tried to look more relaxed than she felt. But the truth was, she was more nervous than she had ever been with a man. Even Brent had never affected her this way.

"Something wrong?"

She looked up at Matt. "Wrong?"

Icy water hit her calves, and she gasped, startled. It swirled up around her knees, drenching her rolled-up pants. She jerked her hands out of her pockets and tried desperately to steady herself, but the only solid thing to cling to was Matt. She staggered against him and felt his strong arm come firmly around her waist, his hand spreading across the small of her back.

Heat shot through her body as he pulled her against his hard length and laughed down at her, his eyes dancing. "Is this one of those sneakers you were talking about earlier?"

"Yes," she managed to gasp, breathless. She put her hands against his biceps to push herself away, but his hold tightened inexorably.

"Hang on, Annie. It's going out again."

Desire sucked more strongly at her than the powerful wave as it receded. The sea pulled. Sensations flowed warmly inside her as she looked up at Matt. Her feet sank into the sand.

"I . . . I'm sorry," she murmured, gaining her freedom at last. She put her cold palms to her warm cheeks as she gazed up at him, trying to hide the color in her face. "I didn't see it coming."

"Don't apologize. Neither did I, but I'm glad it did come."

She swung around, her eyes wide. *"Katie!"*

"She's fine. The wave broke up on the rocks over there."

"Thank God," Annie murmured, spotting her daughter.

Matt brushed her braid back over her shoulder and she jumped. Why did he keep touching her? He smiled ruefully. "Sorry I startled you. You have beautiful hair, Annie. Most women these days cut it short or wear one of those mop styles."

"I think I'd better go down and stay closer to Katie," she said warily.

He searched her eyes. "Fine. Let's go."

"You don't need to come. Why don't you just relax and enjoy the sun?"

He laughed softly. "Still trying to get rid of me?" He began walking down the waterline toward Katie, and Annie had little choice but to go along. After a moment he looked at her. "Don't be afraid of me, Annie."

"I'm not afraid." He was too close. Her shoulder was almost brushing against his bicep. Every time she moved away, he closed the distance within a few steps. She moved again, and he gave her a glance that was both amused and solemn.

"But I make you nervous, right?"

Nervous was exactly what she felt. Also, intensely aware of his masculinity, threatened by her own stirred emotions, aroused by his touch, afraid of just what he wanted from her.

"A little, yes," she admitted.

"Mommy! Matt! Come quick before it gets away!" Katie cried, waving excitedly. Annie, thankful for the

44

distraction, began to jog down the beach.

Matt's easy lope kept pace with her stride. "What do you suppose she's found?"

She laughed. "Could be anything. She's always coming home with her pockets full."

Katie was prodding something against the rocks with a stick. "There! See it?"

Annie squatted down to get a closer look. "A crab. Oh, he's a big one, all right."

"Can you catch him for me? Please?"

"Not on your life," Annie said, laughing.

"Chicken," Matt teased. He stooped down. "Let's have that poker, Katie." She relinquished it immediately, and he worked it carefully behind the crab, forcing it out into the open.

"Look out," Annie warned as he reached into the water and tried to grab it. He caught it from behind and lifted it. The big pincers opened wide for an attack, the creature's eyes turning around to get a look at its captor.

"He's *ugly!*" Katie grimaced.

"Not to another crab," Matt said, chuckling. "Don't want to keep him?"

"Absolutely not," Annie told him.

"Too small for eating. Back you go buddy." Matt put the crab back into the tidepool, and they watched it scramble frantically sideways to the nearest crack and jam itself in so that it was hardly visible.

Matt straightened and opened his palm toward Katie. "How about this instead?" Lying in his hand was a small shell from which peeped a hermit crab.

"Oh!" Katie reached for it. "Super!"

"You can't keep it, Katie," Annie reminded her. "It belongs in the sea. If you take it from its home, it'll die."

"I know," Katie said. She took the shell carefully.

Matt smiled at Annie, his eyes glowing. "Sometimes the same thing is true of people," he said cryptically. Annie wondered what he meant.

Katie stood up and took his hand. "Will you take me out to see the really good tidepools, Matt?"

He glanced at Annie for approval. She hesitated, then nodded. She followed closely after them, then lagged behind to watch. She had never seen Katie take to anyone the way she was taking to this stranger. Annie watched her daughter pointing things out to Matt, who spoke to her, then laughed at her remark.

Annie knew Katie longed for a father. Her questions kept cropping up, questions Annie didn't want to answer just yet, questions she wasn't even sure she ever could answer with complete honesty.

Katie and Matt were some distance away. "That's far enough, I think," she called out to them.

"It's okay, Mommy. Matt's with me!" But he had only to say something to her, and she reached up to him. Annie watched as he swung Katie effortlessly up onto his shoulders and held her little hands high as he started back. Katie's gangly legs dangled over his shoulders. Her face was beaming.

Annie's heart constricted as she watched Matt tread

his way carefully. "Don't worry. I'm not going to drop her," he reassured her.

Annie followed them up the sandy beach, and watched his back muscles ripple beneath his snug safari shirt as he swung Katie to the ground. He leaned over to say something to her, and she darted up the beach, her pigtails flying.

"Where's she going?" Annie asked.

"She's going to check our coals. I wanted a few minutes alone with you." He looked at her closely. "Why were you so upset a minute ago?"

"I wasn't upset."

He looked faintly impatient, but didn't press the issue. They walked together for a while. "She's a nice little girl."

"Yes, she is. She's also very sensitive."

He raised his brows slightly. "Meaning?"

Annie bit down on her lower lip, not sure how to explain, or even if she should. What could she say? That he was only going to be at Makawsa for a few days, and she didn't want him to encourage Katie's affection?

"Does she spend much time with her father?" Matt asked, startling her with his sensitivity to her thoughts.

"No." She doubted if Brent even knew Katie's birthday. "As a matter of fact, she doesn't see him at all."

Now, why had she told him that? It didn't concern him. She glanced up and saw the questioning look in his eyes.

47

"It's ready!" Katie called farther up the beach. "I'm hungry. Can we eat now?"

"I'll bet you're always hungry," Matt called back.

Annie didn't want to like him, but she found herself responding to his warmth. It was enough to make her wary.

In spite of her protests, Matt barbecued the hamburgers. She had to be content ladling out potato salad and fixing buns according to request: Katie, ketchup; Matt, the works. The corn was done first, and she gingerly unrolled Katie's from the tinfoil and sprinkled it lightly with salt.

"You know, I should be doing all this," she told Matt as he flipped the hamburgers on his grate. Katie, who was already almost finished with her corn, was watching the meat cook.

"You can do the dishes," he said.

Katie giggled. "There aren't any dishes, silly. We're using paper plates."

"Bright kid." Matt scooped a hamburger dramatically off the grill and slid it onto Katie's bun. "Young ladies first."

"It's not charred. Boy, am I glad you're cooking!"

Annie pretended to take a swing at her. Katie ducked and laughed. Holding her plate out, Annie said, "Old ladies second?"

"Beautiful ladies," he corrected, his eyes warmly teasing.

Before Annie was half done, Katie was finished. She jumped up. "Can we make the sand castle now?"

"You start on the foundations, and I'll be down in a few minutes," Annie told her. Katie dashed down the beach with her small bucket and shovel.

Annie sat with Matt, eating in silence, feeling uneasy with herself. "You're a very good chef, Mr. Hagen," she said finally, needing to say something.

"I've had a little practice in the last sixteen months. I've been cooking out a good deal."

"Sixteen months?" she repeated in surprise.

"I decided to treat myself to a longtime fantasy. I quit working, bought the van, and took off across the country. I've been traveling the blue roads on the map instead of the main highways."

Oh, Lord, Annie thought, not one of those. "You don't look forty."

"Pardon me? I'm thirty-five. Do I look forty?" He laughed.

"I've heard it's usually about that age that men go through a midlife crisis."

"You mean when they begin having mental break-downs from high-stress jobs and start buying fast cars and taking seventeen-year-old girl friends?" he asked, his mouth twitching.

"Something like that. Or were you just burned out?"

"Not quite, but I knew I didn't want to keep going the way I had been. I needed time to think."

Sixteen months to think?

She could sure pick them. The first man she had been attracted to in five years, and he was a bum, or close to it. It didn't do her self-esteem much good to

49

realize that seven years of reality hadn't improved her perceptiveness one iota. The slacks and nice sports jacket he had worn were probably remnants from a relatively responsible, respectable past.

Feeling him watching her, she glanced up. His gaze was fixed on her mouth. She took a shaky sip of Coke, wishing he would watch the ocean, the sea gulls, Katie, the low burning coals, anything except her. Forcing her eyes from his, Annie looked down the beach to where Katie was digging contentedly in the sand.

"What does Makawsa mean?" Matt asked casually, taking another bite of his hamburger.

"It's a Pomo Indian word meaning Salmon-ridge people," she told him, relaxing on this neutral ground. "The tribe had a village not far from where our farmhouse is now, so I adopted the word."

"And Gualala?"

"Our little town?" She smiled. "Same origins. It means water-coming-down place." She laughed. "If you mention Gualala anywhere other than the Mendocino coast, people will think you're talking about someplace in Mexico."

Matt stretched out on his side and raised himself partly on one elbow. His gaze moved leisurely over her face, as though memorizing each feature. "Are you a native of the area?"

"A transplant. I'm a native Californian, but I was raised in San Diego. I came north to go to Berkeley, then moved up here with Katie after—" She stopped herself abruptly, realizing with something akin to shock just how much of her life story she was blurting out.

"After what?"

"Pardon?"

"You said you were raised in San Diego, came north to Berkeley for college and then moved up here *after . . .*" He left the sentence hanging, waiting with obvious interest for her to finish it.

"I'm boring you." She quickly stacked the paper plates and shoved them back into the picnic basket, then took out the marshmallows and roasting skewers.

Matt sat up slowly, watching her. He rested his forearms on his raised knees. "Annie, you couldn't bore me if you tried."

She stood up quickly, shaken by the look in his blue eyes. He stood up, too. Her heart jumped, then raced wildly as he came around the campfire to stand directly in front of her. She moved back. "I . . . I promised to make a sandcastle with Katie," she said quickly, immediately feeling like one of her daughter's second-grade friends.

Matt didn't push. "Fine. Let's go."

She didn't want him to come with her. She wanted space between them. "I'm sure you didn't plan to spend your afternoon digging in the sand."

"I didn't expect to see you standing in the middle of a flower garden either. And I haven't poked through tidepools in a long time. In fact, I have a feeling I'm going to enjoy a lot of things I haven't enjoyed in years. Like making sandcastles."

He wasn't even trying to be subtle. If she was going to get her point across, she would have to be equally clear with him.

"You look ready for battle," he observed ruefully.

"Look, Mr. Hagen, I'm not exactly sure why you came back to Makawsa—"

"Yes, you are, Annie."

Fresh air everywhere and she couldn't draw a single deep breath. Defensive anger rose. "Room and board for three nights is all you're going to get at Makawsa, *Mr.* Hagen."

His expression softened. "Do you dislike every man who's attracted to you? Or is it something in particular about me?"

"It's you," she said frankly before thinking better of it.

"The van? The beard I shaved off? Or that I'm not going to dissemble about coming on to you?"

She drew a sharp breath. "All of that!"

"Then let's talk about it," he suggested, coming closer and reaching out to rest his hand lightly on her shoulder, his thumb caressing the sensitive curve of her neck. Warmth surged through her veins at his touch. "Annie," he murmured, looking squarely into her wary eyes, "I want to know everything about you, from your birth on. What do you need to know about me to feel safe enough to talk to me?" She felt her resistance melting and steeled herself from giving in to him. "If you only knew how long I've been looking for you," he whispered, his head lowering slowly.

Brent had once said something very similar. Annie snapped out of her trance and stepped back. "I don't need to know *anything* about you," she said tautly.

"Nothing?" he challenged, his eyes searching hers intently.

She was certain Matt Hagen was worldly enough to know exactly what he was doing to her. It was probably why he was doing it. His money must be running out, and he needed an easy touch. Pay for the weekend stay, seduce a lonely, love-starved divorceé, and prolong the visit to a few weeks. Gratis, of course.

"I know everything I need to know about you already," she said coolly.

He frowned. "Such as?"

"You've paid for your room and board, and you'll be leaving Makawsa Monday morning." She turned away with determination and headed down the beach toward Katie.

The last thing she expected was for her daughter to join forces against her. "Matt! Come help build the sandcastle!"

"Katie, just leave the man alone, will you please?" she pleaded. "I'm sure he's got better things to do."

Katie stared at her out of wide, hurt eyes. "He liked looking in the tidepools. I could tell." Annie felt miserable. She didn't want to take her tension out on Katie. "Don't you like him, Mommy? I think he's just *super!*"

Annie could see that plainly enough. Katie's smile glowed even brighter. Annie clenched her teeth. Oh, why had she ever allowed Matt Hagen to stay. She'd known instinctively from the first that he was trouble.

"Mommy's good at turrets," Katie was saying to Matt as he approached, "but you can help me dig the moats."

"Yes, ma'am," he said with amusement. He squatted down and glanced across at Annie with a faint, taunting smile. "Turrets, hmm? Appropriate enough, I'd say. Tell me, are there guards at the draw-bridge, too? Alligators in the moat? How does a good man breach the castle walls?"

Annie's mouth tightened angrily.

"We built an office building last time," Katie informed him, using her trowel to toss sand to one side. "Just like the one my daddy works in."

"Oh?" Matt replied, his expression one of open interest. "What's he do for a living?"

Annie glared at him.

"He hides money for people," Katie told him seriously. Annie's mouth dropped open.

Matt laughed. "Sounds like an interesting profession."

"Oh, he's very good at it," Katie boasted.

"Katie, your father's an attorney," Annie repeated for the hundredth time. "He specializes in corporate law and finding tax shelters for wealthy people."

"But when I asked you what that meant, you told me he hid money so people wouldn't have to pay taxes on it."

Said in just that way, it sounded not only immoral

but also illegal. "It's a very good profession, Katie, and perfectly . . . respectable." To some people, Annie added mentally.

Matt hadn't missed her hesitation.

She lowered her eyes from his and concentrated on the turret again. She thought of Brent, who had begun law school with grand ideals. He was going to be a public defender to help those who couldn't afford a big-name lawyer. Then . . .

"He lives in New York City," Katie went on, Matt listening. "He owns a great big hundred-story office building on Fifth Avenue, and his office is right on top so he can look down on everybody."

Annie couldn't believe what she was hearing.

"He must be a very important person," Matt said seriously, not looking at Annie.

"Oh, he is," Katie insisted. "He has lunch with the president and flies to Disney World every weekend."

Annie stared at her daughter in dismay. Katie caught her look and lowered her eyes.

"I think the moat needs to be deeper, don't you, Katie?" Annie asked gently. "And aren't we going to need some driftwood for the drawbridge?"

Katie looked up briefly, her eyes bright with unshed tears. She nodded silently, got up, and walked down the beach. Annie sensed Matt looking at them and couldn't meet his gaze. She worked on the turret until it was finished.

"You'll have to move so I can do the last one," she said.

He moved just enough to allow her space to work, but he'd brought one knee up, and his body almost brushed hers. "A recent divorce?"

"Seven and a half years." She was doing it again. He asked, she answered. Even though it was none of his business.

He didn't say anything for a while, and she wasn't about to go on talking. She felt uneasy under his scrutiny.

"That's a long time, Annie. Time enough to be over it. But you're still hanging onto something of it, aren't you? Are you still in love with your husband?"

"I'm over *him,*" she said pointedly. "But I learned quite a lot from the experience."

Brent had shattered her. It had taken her a long time to put the pieces back together. And now this man had come along—handsome, compelling, charming, and "coming on to her." "Look, Mr. Hagen, I have no intention of ever getting involved with another man. Is that clear enough for you?"

"Very clear," he said seriously. "It's going to be up to me to change your mind, isn't it?" He reached out, cupping the nape of her neck firmly in his large palm, and pulled her toward him as he bent his head.

She gasped, too stunned to protest, and then the opportunity was lost, for his mouth was covering hers. Her muscles jerked at the first shocking contact.

His kiss was firm, long, declarative, and intensely arousing. His other hand moved up along her arm, resting gently on her shoulder as his thumb traced the line of her sensitive collarbone. How could he know that was one of her most vulnerable, erotic points? Her breasts tingled, waiting for that warm hand to descend and spread the good feelings. But it remained where it was, tormentingly near. Oh, God, it felt so good . . .

His tongue lightly stroked her upper lip, probing no deeper than the edge of her teeth, then penetrating, lightly touching her tongue. She moaned softly, tilting her head back, and his kiss became demanding, fiery.

When he finally drew back, his breath was coming hard and fast. "Oh, Annie . . ." he whispered hoarsely, his eyes dark with desire.

She panted softly, stunned. Staring up at him, she drew back as though he had scorched her. "You had no right," she choked out, frightened by the impact of that kiss.

"No, I didn't," he admitted with apology. "But I wanted to."

Her eyes burned with the wild tumult of her emotions. Her heart raced even faster at the smoldering look in his blue eyes. She edged away from him. She had read once that people who were chaste for long periods of time shook violently when sexually aroused. She couldn't stop shaking. She was afraid she was going to burst out crying right here in front of him and make a complete fool of herself.

He, on the other hand, seemed in full control of himself.

Angry and frightened, she attacked. "And you're undoubtedly one of those men who does exactly *what* he wants, *when* he wants, *no matter* what anyone feels about it, aren't you?"

His brows flickered up. "I wouldn't go quite so far as that," he answered, "but I've always believed a person should act on his instincts."

She knew what instincts he was acting on! "Then perhaps I should act on mine!"

His clear gaze penetrated her. "The instincts that are telling you to send me packing for fear of being hurt again? Or those that were in play a few moments ago when you kissed me back?"

Her face burned. "I meant what I said."

"We're already involved, Annie, and you know it. We were the minute we saw each other."

She was about to deny it vehemently when a loud noise startled her. "Here's the wood, Mommy," Katie said, standing beside a dozen small pieces of driftwood. Annie wondered anxiously how much Katie had heard or seen. She clenched her hands tightly, half expecting an embarrassing question.

But Katie said nothing. She looked from Annie to Matt curiously. Matt smiled wryly and left it to Annie to say something, but she couldn't. Finally she forced a smile and managed to say, "Well, don't just stand there, honey. Let's finish the castle." She bent forward and went back to work, trying to ignore the fact that both Katie and Matt were watching her intently.

As soon as they got back to Makawsa, she'd return

his money and send him packing, she decided. She had to before anything else happened.

4

"MOMMY ALWAYS SAYS the sun kisses the ocean good night just before it leaves," Katie said as they sat near the fire waiting for sunset. "Then it kisses it again each morning when it comes back." Katie looked at Matt. "Do you believe that, Matt?"

He slid a roasted marshmallow off a skewer and ate it. "That's a nice way of putting it," he said, glancing at Annie.

"It's not the truth, though," Katie told him. "I used to believe all that when I was little, but then Mrs. Gilroy told our class that the sun is really millions and billions of miles away. And it doesn't kiss anything. All those colors are really air pol . . . pollu . . ."

"Pollutants?" Matt supplied.

"Yes. Smog makes a pretty sunset," Katie said, full of self-importance at imparting this bit of knowledge.

Annie stared at her daughter in amazement. "I didn't know you learned that."

Katie shrugged. "Well, you always like telling me that story."

"What else do you know?" Matt asked.

"Oh, everything. Just ask me," Katie announced with all the confidence of the very young.

"All right. How deep is the ocean?"

Katie giggled. "*Very* deep. It's very *wide* too. See?" she said smugly.

"You have a smart-aleck daughter, Annie," Matt said, chuckling.

The easy camaraderie between them disturbed Annie. Katie wasn't around a great many adults, and those she did meet usually made her shy. She was polite, quiet, nothing else. But this attraction to Matt was different. She responded to Matt naturally, as though they'd known each other for a long time. It was worrisome.

Katie yawned widely and stretched like a young cat. Annie took her opportunity. "Time to head for home, young lady," she announced, standing up.

Katie groaned. "Awww, Mommy . . ."

Annie gathered together the last of the cookout things. Matt shoveled sand over the coals.

With the sunset behind them, they climbed up the trail. Katie let the way, talking the whole time. Annie followed, Matt close behind her. Once when she paused, he put his hand lightly on her hip. "Easy," he whispered when she jumped in surprise, his expression gently reproving. After that, she kept several steps ahead of him.

"It's sky-blue-pink," Katie said when they reached the top and looked back. Great swirls of pink streaked the blue sky. Matt stood just below Annie on the last few feet of the trail. He looked at her, not interested in the sunset.

"Thanks for letting me come along," he said as they approached the van.

"We were glad to have you," she replied politely, not meeting his eyes. Katie was watching them with smiling interest, which embarrassed Annie all the more. Matt unlocked the door, and Katie got into the back.

"We should get a van, Mommy," she said. "We could go down to San Francisco and sleep in it instead of a hotel. Then the trip wouldn't cost much."

Annie glanced at Matt, and then back at her daughter. "You're forgetting we'd have to buy the van first."

That fact didn't register on Katie's enthusiasm. "Matt can even listen to tapes, can't you?" Katie boasted. "Can we hear some now?"

"Katie!" Annie scolded.

Matt reached down and snapped open a cassette case. After a brief search, he plucked out a tape and slipped it into the tape deck.

Annie heard the first familiar words and her face warmed until it felt as if it was on fire. She turned away and stared out the window, her hands clenched. John Denver's voice floated through the van as he sang "Annie's Song."

"Matt, do you like my mom?" Katie asked bluntly, and Annie's head snapped around to give Katie a quelling look. Katie looked at her in surprise. "Why's your face so red?"

Matt chuckled softly. "Because she *knows* I like her, Kitten."

"Oh, *good.* There was this one man who came to our house last summer. He followed her everywhere all the time."

"Katie, that's enough, please."

"He liked her a lot, too. He tried to kiss her once down by the barn. I saw. But she—"

"Young lady, sometimes I think you talk just to be sure your lips won't grow together," Annie said in vexation, her face so hot she was sure Matt could feel it from where he sat. Katie's mouth opened. Annie gave her a half-pleading, half-warning look. Katie closed her mouth and she said nothing more.

Matt pulled into the Makawsa driveway. As soon as he stopped the van, Annie opened her door. "Bath and then bed, Katie," she said firmly, in no mood for arguments. Katie capitulated with amazing speed, throwing her arms around Annie's neck and kissing her before jumping down from the van. "Thanks for the cookout, Mommy." She ran up the stairs and paused at the top. "See you in the house, Matt." After unlocking the door with Annie's key, leaving it in the lock, she banged into the house.

Annie reached into the van for the wicker basket and the bag of charcoal, but Matt had come around and reached past her at the same time. He brushed against her, and she moved quickly to one side.

"I can get them," she told him stiffly. She clutched the basket defensively, but he put his hand on hers and stood squarely in her way.

"Let's not make it a power struggle." He took the

basket from her and set it to one side. "Now, say it and get it behind us."

"Say what?" she demanded angrily.

"Whatever it is that's eating you most."

This was the time. He was asking for it. She took a deep breath. "All right. I think it would be best if you left."

He didn't look surprised or angry. He rested his hand on the van roof just above her right shoulder, effectively penning her in. "Spell out why."

She became increasingly, uncomfortably aware of his well-formed body, of the darkness of his eyes, of his mouth curving very slightly. Her muscles grew tense. She found it difficult to breathe.

"A lot of reasons," she hedged, knowing full well that the primary one was just what he was making her feel right now: desire, vulnerability.

He studied her face and held her gaze again. "It's too late to turn me out, Annie," he told her, his voice deeper.

"It's early yet," she said quickly, deliberately mis-understanding what he meant.

He leaned closer, his mouth inches from hers. "Would you have me scouring the coast for a place to spend the night?"

Her heart knocked crazily against her ribs. "You have your van."

"I was looking forward to stretching out in a real bed," he said. He reached out and gently touched her cheek. "Annie, you've got nothing to worry about. I won't try to steal into your bed at midnight, though I'll probably dream about it."

He leaned so close that she froze, but he was just picking up the basket and charcoal. "Would you mind sliding the door shut for me?" he asked calmly.

He was *staying.*

Surely three nights wouldn't turn her world upside down. She was stronger than that, surely. She slid the van door closed with a bang.

Matt was waiting for her on the front steps. "Do you ever sit outside on your porch?"

"Sometimes. It's too cold this evening." She didn't look at him.

As soon as he opened the front door screen for her, she heard the bathwater running like Niagara Falls. "Oh!" she gasped. "Just put the things anywhere. Excuse me!" She raced down the hallway and poked her head into the steam-filled bathroom. "Katie! Turn off that water. I think you have enough to sink the *Bismark.*"

The claw-footed tub was mounted high with Mr. Bubble. "Is that one *capful?*" she exclaimed.

"Oh! I thought it was one *cupful,*" Katie said, grinning broadly as she peeped out at one end, the cascading roar dying as she cranked the faucets off.

So much for hot water, Annie thought grimly. At least until much later.

As she neared the kitchen, she saw that the basket was no longer in the hallway. Matt was standing with the refrigerator door open, putting away a small jar of mayonnaise. "She okay?" he asked.

"She's fine. But if you were hoping for a hot shower, you're going to have to wait an hour or so. I'm sorry."

He closed the refrigerator door and leaned back against it, his arms crossed. "I'd guessed that already by the way you ran down that hall. No matter," he added, straightening. His eyes danced over her. "I was planning on a cold one anyway."

Ignoring him, she went about putting away the rest of the things. "Will you be turning in soon?" she asked.

He glanced at the sunflower wall clock. "It's only seven. Past my bedtime, too?" His expression was amused.

"I didn't mean—" She stopped. He knew she hadn't meant that. "If you would like a fire in the living room fireplace, there's one laid and ready. You're free to sit there if you like." Her expression told him to go, now.

He leaned against the kitchen counter, not two feet from where she was standing. He watched her hands. She tried to keep them steady as she lifted out the ketchup bottle and pickles. "Do you watch television?" he asked.

"No. The reception is nil without a disk up here, so we don't even have one."

"Good. A little music, then, and some conversation. That's what appeals to me," he murmured softly.

"Radio or records. *No* tapes," she told him, hoping the effect of his suggestion didn't show in her eyes.

"Don't you like John Denver?"

65

She took out the dirty paper plates and napkins and dumped them into the garbage can under the counter. She removed the cloth lining to be washed and went to replace the basket in the pantry.

Matt followed, leaning indolently in the doorway, watching her stretch on her tiptoes to slide the basket back onto a high shelf. His eyes moved slowly down the full length of her body and back up again. She snapped off the light, hiding herself in darkness.

His silhouette remained immobile in front of her, blocking the doorway. Warm tendrils of desire snaked her as she observed the shape of his large, virile body framed against the light. She pressed her hand to her stomach to stop the quivering.

"Annie?" His tone was soft, husky, questioning. He stepped forward into the darkened room, and she realized with a jolt what her silence might be construed to mean.

"Excuse me," she said quickly, brushing past him. "I have to check on Katie." She left the kitchen as quickly as she could, aware of him staring after her with a faint frown.

Katie was still soaking in the tub, playing with the suds. "Look, I'm Santa Claus!" she announced, a sudsy beard hanging from her chin.

"Time you were out, sweetheart," Annie told her, setting her woolly pajamas with Strawberry Shortcake out on the bathroom counter and spreading toothpaste on Katie's toothbrush.

"Your face is all funny, Mommy. You always tell me I have a fever when I'm hot."

She did have a fever, a fever in her blood! Was Matt Hagen still in her kitchen? She hoped he would just go down the hall to his room and stay there.

"Where's Matt?"

"Never mind Matt," Annie said too sharply. "You're going to bed."

"I still get my story, don't I?" Katie asked plaintively.

Annie softened. "Yes. If you get out of the tub right now, before you turn into a prune."

She kept thinking about Matt standing in the pantry doorway and remembering his kiss on the beach. She heard him go down the hall and relaxed slightly when his door closed. *Just stay there, Mr. Hagen, and leave me well enough alone.*

Katie put on her pajamas and went to get *Charlotte's Web.* Annie set a match to the fire in the living room and put on *Mystic Moods,* glad that Matt was out of the way so she could have this quiet, private time with Katie. It was the best part of her day, and she cherished it.

Sitting down on the couch, she snuggled Katie close and opened the book. She'd just finished reading a chapter aloud when Matt walked in, wearing clean but faded blue jeans and a lightweight blue sweater. Her pulse leaped sharply. Matt looked at them and frowned. "Why are you both crying?"

Annie quickly wiped away her tears. Katie sniffed loudly. "Charlotte"—sniff—"just died."

"Who's Charlotte?" he asked, looking at Annie. "A relative?"

"A spider."

If he laughed, she'd kick him. But he didn't, surprising her yet again. He smiled slightly, but not in amusement or mockery.

The telephone rang, rescuing her from trying to figure him out. Did she want to anyway? Best to keep distance between them in all ways.

John Bollington from the Santa Rosa toy outlet was calling to order two dozen more elephant puzzles. The last batch had sold like hot cakes, he said. Especially the pink ones, which seemed to be very popular. Could she finish the order in two weeks? She told him she would try, but she had a mini-wreath order to complete for the Fort Bragg store and some matted wildflower watercolors to do for Jenner-by-the-Sea and the Gualala General Store.

When she returned to the living room, she found Katie curled up comfortably on Matt's lap in the easy chair, listening to another chapter of *Charlotte's Web*. His long, hard, muscled legs were out and his bare feet were propped up on her hassock. He was certainly making himself right at home.

"It's bedtime, Katie."

"Just one more chapter. It's at a good part."

"The whole book is 'a good part.' Now off to bed, honey."

"Awww . . ." Katie groaned in open rebellion, looking at Matt for assistance.

"Do what your mother says," he told her, straightening her up off his lap and giving her a light swat on the behind. "See you in the morning." To Annie's amazement, Katie smiled brightly at him, kissed him on the cheek, and went without another word.

Annie felt a rush of almost blinding resentment. She didn't like the way he looked so relaxed in her living room. More to the point, she didn't like the way he looked at *her* and made her feel certain he understood exactly what she was feeling.

He leaned back comfortably. "Come back, Annie, and we'll talk after you've tucked her in for the night."

Assuming she wanted to talk! Usually when a guest seemed to want company, she complied politely, whatever her work load. But not this time! She was afraid that spending time with this man would put a mark on her she'd never be able to erase.

"I'm sorry, but I have some work I have to get done."

He said nothing, but his expression grew enigmatic.

"The telephone call," she felt compelled to add. It was the truth, but she knew she was avoiding his company because it stirred her. Worse, she knew *he* knew. "You can change the record if you want," she suggested finally, not knowing what else to say. "There are more records in the cabinet over by the window. If you get hungry, please feel free to help yourself in the kitchen. There are fresh oatmeal cookies in the Winnie-the-Pooh jar."

His mouth curved faintly, his eyes gently mocking her.

"Good night, Mr. Hagen." She turned away and escaped down the hall to Katie's room to say prayers, dispense kisses and hugs, and switch out the light.

Annie went into her workroom and was standing at the table making a quick inventory of what she needed to complete her mini-wreaths when Matt pushed the door open. She glanced up sharply.

"You were serious about working," he said, coming in without an invitation.

"You could at least knock. This could have been my bedroom!"

"The door was ajar, and I could see it wasn't a bedroom," he said, undaunted. His mouth curved. "Besides, Katie told me your bedroom is the first door on the left, right next to the hall to the kitchen."

Had he asked or had Katie volunteered that information? Annie wondered.

Matt looked around the room, taking in the shelves filled with craft materials—unstained plaques, boxes of pine-cones, seeds, dried pits, supplies of water-colors, chalks, acrylics in tubes, files of folk art designs, an empty easel leaning against the back wall, and boxes stacked with completed projects awaiting delivery.

"Then this is your real livelihood and not Makawsa's guests?"

"Yes. But rent on the room helps a great deal."

He pulled a stool over to the table and sat down. He

studied several ink sketches of Fort Ross. "These are very good. Did you have training?"

"I was an art major at Berkeley for two years. I quit shortly after I married." She looked down at her work-table, hoping to avoid further questions, and hoping he would take the hint and leave.

Matt set the sketches down. "What are you going to work on this evening?" he asked, crossing his fore-arms and leaning against the table.

"Two dozen mini-wreaths and a few folk art plaques," she said, managing enough control of her trembling fingers to finish tying on her apron. She also had to draw elephant patterns onto squares of wood before she could use her jigsaw in the barn shop in the morning. Enough to keep her busy past mid-night again.

Matt was smiling at her. "I'll keep you company." Her lips parted in protest. "You're going to tell me again that I'd be more interested doing something else, right? Well, I wouldn't be."

"Stay if you want to," she said grimly, "but don't expect any scintillating conversation from me. I can't work and talk at the same time." She scraped her stool closer to the table and sat down, rearranging boxes of seeds and redwood pinecones within easier reach. She laid out six small wooden bases and reached for her glue gun.

Matt leaned close. "You need more light." He pressed the switch on her goose necked lamp. This close, she could smell the faint musky aftershave he wore and the special scent that was *him*. If someone could bottle it, they'd make a million. She tried to relax, but her fingers felt stiff, clumsy, and cold with an attack of nerves.

"When I was driving through the Ozarks," Matt began, "I met an old man who made wooden toys." He talked easily of his travels, the people he'd met, places he'd seen. Gradually his calm, easy going manner helped her relax. She even laughed with him several times over anecdotes he shared. She liked his laugh, the way his eyes glowed and the way they crinkled at the corners, and the grooves cut deeply into his cheeks. When he laughed, she felt it was coming from inside him, unforced and spontaneous.

Wiping her hands off carefully, she checked over the finished wreaths, surprised at how quickly the work had gone. She warned him to stay back while she sprayed varnish over them and added the last few touches of bright red porcelain berries. He watched her move the tray aside.

"How many of those things do you make?"

"Three thousand last year," she said, with a faint self-mocking laugh.

"I hope you get a good price for them."

"A dollar apiece. The stores sell them for about three."

"I suggest you raise your price."

"I've been thinking about it." She shrugged. "When I get really sick of making them, I'll try something else for a while." She set out half a dozen plaques, stained, lightly varnished, and with folk art patterns already transferred onto them. She sat down again, pulling her paint box over and dipping two empty cottage cheese containers into the bucket of water she kept under the table.

"What now?" he asked, interested.

She laid out several brushes. "This is tole work. One-stroke painting. People used to use it on tin. Now you can put it on just about everything." She sighed heavily, straightening and shifting her aching shoulders.

Matt stood up and came around the table. "I bet you could use a neck massage."

She glanced up at him, her heart thundering. "No, I—"

"Come on, Annie, relax." He put his large, warm hands on her shoulders and turned her back to face the worktable again. "Am I all that threatening?" he asked softly.

He was. He threatened her peace of mind, revealed her own deep need for human touch, awakened something she had never felt before, something that frightened her with its power. The word *intimacy* had taken on new meaning. It wasn't just physical touch, lovemaking, possession—as it had been with Brent. It was looking into this man's eyes and feeling somehow connected with him in a profound way.

She didn't want this. Life ran more smoothly without complications. Yet the gentle kneading of his fingers sent ripples of pleasure through her body. She gripped the edge of her worktable and tried to think of this as impersonal therapy, all the while sensing instinctively that there was nothing at all impersonal in his touch.

"Why did you travel for so long?" she asked shakily, hoping conversation would help keep her head clear.

"I needed to sort things out, decide what was important. I needed to reevaluate my priorities." She heard the faint husky timbre of his voice and knew that touching her was affecting him, too.

"And did you sort things out?"

"Yes. It was a long time coming 'round, but I worked through it." His hands stopped. "Turn around, Annie."

She went very still, her heart beating wildly like a trapped bird's. "Why?" She swiveled slowly on the stool, facing him.

"I want to look at you," he whispered. His hands began their slow, tormenting, tantalizing massage again, sending messages she was frightened to decipher but really didn't need to. He tipped up her chin, and she saw the velvety darkness of his widening pupils. Her pulse throbbed warmly, every sense in her body alive.

"The first lesson everyone should learn is how to relax," he whispered, bending slowly to kiss her. He barely brushed her mouth with his own. "People don't seem to realize"—he kissed her again—"that it's a *learned* process"—and again—"like any other."

Each feathery touch drove her heartbeat higher until her lips parted on a softly indrawn breath that caught in her throat. Then he lightly caressed her upper lip, teasing her lips open. Desire bloomed hot and heavy inside her.

Oh, Matt Hagen, kiss me the way you did at the beach, she thought, trembling. She put her hands up against his chest, feeling the hard muscles, the heat, the strength, the hard, fast pounding of his heart.

Cupping her face with his hands, he raised his head to look down at her. She saw her own passion mirrored in his darkened eyes. He took her hands, drawing her up. Slowly he draped them over his shoulders and slid his arms around her.

"This is a mistake," she murmured softly, fighting for reason even as she stepped forward.

"No," he whispered roughly, lifting her chin again so that she had to look at him. "This is the only right thing that's ever happened to either one of us."

This time when he kissed her, he parted her lips and took her mouth in a way that left no doubt that he wanted her. Not just with his body, for she knew that by the hard length of him pressed provocatively against her, but with a consuming need that shook every preconceived belief she had about passion. It was sunlight at midnight, magic when she had left fantasy behind, consummation of sense and senses.

He lifted his mouth from hers. She could hear their heightened breathing. "I love how you taste, Annie," he murmured, kissing her again. "Clean, warm, so sweet . . ." His mouth moved tenderly against the arched, slender column of her throat, nibbling and lightly sucking along the taut cords, drawing a soft moan from her.

"Matt . . ."

His hands arched her back as he rubbed seductively against her, and her body responded with a natural pulsing movement that drew a sharp exhalation from him. His hands tightened; his kiss grew fevered. She tilted her face up to meet his kiss, and he uttered a muted groan against her lips. He caught her arms, pulling them down, and then stepped back from her.

He made no effort to hide what he felt. His face was tense and sweat glistened on his brow. He was breathing heavily. "I'd better let you go now," he murmured hoarsely, "or I won't be able to at all." Lightly he stroked her cheek, smiling ruefully. "We already know this about each other, don't we? Mutual attraction, though that's not quite strong enough to describe it. There are a lot of other things to know before we act on it." He kissed her tenderly on the forehead. "Good night, Annie."

Closing her eyes tightly, she listened to him leave. He was right, but the denial should have come from her. Why didn't it seem to matter?

How would she feel in the morning, looking at him across the breakfast table and knowing that, if he hadn't put an end to it, she would willingly have been backward over her worktable for him to finish what he had started?

Oh, God, what was happening to her? Why couldn't she think about that blue van and him wandering around for sixteen months? Why couldn't she focus on Katie and how she might get hurt?

Annie raised a trembling hand to her mouth, which was swollen from Matt's impassioned kisses, and felt the burn of unexpected tears. How long had it been since she had let herself cry?

She had work to do! What was the sense of standing here in a daze, yearning for something, for someone who she knew would shatter her, just as she had been shattered before? She had put the pieces of herself back together once. She couldn't go through that kind of pain again. She had Katie. She didn't *need* anyone else. Why get involved at all? She had her friends here at Gualala. They were enough.

Sitting down at her worktable, she pulled over a plaque. Staring down at the words she read: *"I finally got it all together, but I forgot where I put it."*

She sighed, thinking how apropos the saying was. After rolling her brush in red paint, she began to fill in the letters.

5

As usual, Katie climbed into Annie's bed early the next morning to snuggle for a few minutes before getting up. "Do you think Matt's awake yet, Mommy?

"Probably not." Thinking of him just down the hall was unnerving. Annie wondered how he slept. Did he wear pajamas? For some reason, she didn't think so.

"Let's fix him something really good for breakfast," Katie said. "Waffles, or biscuits and cheese eggs."

Annie smiled slightly. "Trying to impress him?"

"It's almost morning. Maybe I should go in—"

"Absolutely not," Annie told her firmly. "Now listen, Katie, he's only here for the weekend, and then he'll be on his way again. Don't get too attached to him." She pushed Katie's hair back from her temples.

"Maybe he'll stay if he likes us."

Annie sighed heavily. "No, he won't."

"Why not?"

"Because we don't take in free boarders," she said with faint annoyance.

"Maybe he has lots and lots of money."

"I doubt it, and it wouldn't matter if he did. I think he just stopped off for a few home-cooked meals and a decent bed to sleep in before going on down the road again."

Katie looked up at her. "Don't you like him, Mommy?"

Annie frowned, drawing her daughter close again. That was just the problem. She did like him. Too much. She just didn't want to get involved with him. "He's our guest, Katie. That's all, and that's how he will be treated."

Annie sent Katie to her room to get dressed while she went into the bathroom to shower. It took almost thirty minutes to blow dry her waist-length hair. Before braiding it, she pulled on jeans and a forest-green sweater she had crocheted and went to check on Katie.

But Katie wasn't in her room, and her bed was still unmade. Annie went to the kitchen. She stared in surprise at the sight of Matt drinking a cup of hot coffee and Katie eating a fried egg and buttered toast at the kitchen table.

"Good morning," he drawled, admiring the fit of her jeans and sweater.

"Matt cooked breakfast," Katie announced, confirming Annie's suspicion.

"Hope you don't mind," he said. "But you did say to make myself at home."

"I was hungry," Katie added.

"No Fruit Loops in the house," Matt said, grinning.

A glance at the wall clock told Annie it was barely seven. "Were you planning on going fishing this morning? If I'd known, I would have gotten up sooner and had everything ready for you."

"I'm not going fishing." He stood up, took a cup and saucer out of the cabinet, and poured her a cup of coffee, which he set on the table opposite him. He drew out a chair for her. She stared at him, her lips slightly parted. After a brief, wary hesitation, she sat down.

Katie finished her last bite of egg and got up, stacking her silverware in preparation for leaving. "I'm going to see Mabel. You wanna come, Matt?"

"Mr. Hagen hasn't had breakfast yet, Katie," Annie told her, then paused. "Have you?"

"I was waiting for you."

Annie looked away. "Before you go out, Katie, you have a bed to make."

"Okay. Come out as soon as you're finished, Matt. I've got lots of things to show you," she chattered. She bolted out of the kitchen, leaving the swinging door going to and fro. Annie stood up.

"Who's Mabel?"

"Her cow. Now, what would you like for breakfast, Mr. Hagen?" she asked, leaving her coffee untouched.

"What's the hurry?"

"Waffles, French toast, bacon and eggs?"

He stretched his hand out on the table. "Annie, sit down," he said quietly.

She was angry. "There's a limit to just how much you can make yourself at home."

His expression softened. "Have you been working up your defenses all night?"

Her cheeks burned. "We won't discuss what happened in my workroom, because it's not going to happen again."

"Annie . . ."

"Waffles, French toast, or bacon and eggs?"

He surveyed her with a wry challenge. "Are the waffles from a box or from scratch?"

Why, when she was being downright rude to him, did he have to give her that gentle smile? "From scratch," she said more calmly, feeling self-conscious.

"Waffles," he said. "That's something I can't fix in my van."

She turned away and began to take the ingredients down from her cupboards. He got up and came to stand near her. After pouring himself more black coffee, he leaned against the counter. "I'm not going to apologize for kissing you last night," he told her over the rim of his cup.

"Why should you?" she said stiffly, not looking at him. She acknowledged her own responsibility in the incident; in fact, by not stopping him, she had invited it. She closed her eyes tightly for a moment, trying to obliterate the memory of his mouth, his hands, his body.

"You shouldn't feel guilty about it either," he said softly.

She glanced sharply up at him. "Let's just forget it altogether," she suggested tightly.

"No, let's not. Let's just see what else we have in common," he said, looking straight into her eyes.

She drew back slightly, feeling that he somehow

loomed closer, though he hadn't moved at all. "You're leaving after the weekend."

"Maybe not. I've got time for a longer stay."

Her heart nearly stopped. "I thought you were seeing the country. You can hardly do that staying here."

"I'm on my way home."

"Where's that?" she asked, hoping to keep the previous suggestion at a distance.

"San Francisco."

"What do you do for a living when you're not traveling, Mr. Hagen?" she asked casually, measuring out the flour and pouring it into a large bowl.

"Live on my laurels," he remarked. "I was in business for myself, but I decided I needed a sabbatical to clear the dust and to see if what I was doing was worth the cost. I decided it wasn't."

She looked up at him. Those few statements opened a trunkful of questions. What laurels had he earned? And how? What kind of business had he been in? What "dust" did he mean, and what cost did he count too much? And, finally, what answers had he sought during his "sabbatical"?

She reminded herself she didn't want to become entangled with this man, and asking questions would get her in deeper. She returned her attention to the waffle batter.

"Chicken," Matt whispered.

"It's none of my business."

"Make it your business, Annie," he said, setting down his coffee cup.

"I don't want to do that," she told him frankly, picking up the bowl and using her whisk to stir the batter. The activity gave vent to her nervous energy and put something solid between them.

"Why not? Wouldn't you like to know something about the man you were kissing?"

She almost dropped the bowl. "That's not fair!"

"Who said anything about playing fair?" He reached out and pushed the thick, heavy fall of braid back from her shoulder. She flinched.

"Don't."

He pushed his hands into the front pockets of his jeans and leaned back against the counter again. "I'll try to curb my natural instincts, Annie. It's just that I've been searching for meaning so long that it's hard to back off when I've finally found something."

She let out a shaky breath and stared up at him, wary. His eyes were so clear and blue, she felt she was drowning in them. She gave a weak laugh. "I'll bet you say that to every woman you meet, Mr. Hagen."

"No, I don't," he told her seriously. "Don't look so scared. It wasn't offered as a threat, just a declaration of intent."

She turned, plunked the bowl down, and bent to get the waffle iron out of a lower cabinet. The sooner she fed him, the sooner he would leave the house and leave her alone.

"Tell me what you're feeling right now," Matt ordered softly. "Let's have everything straight between us from the start. I've had too many relationships in which I had to play mind games."

She straightened and gave him a hard look. "What do you suppose I'm thinking? Some man drives up my road in a dusty, dented van, plunks down enough cash to stay three nights, and then tells me he's found what he's been looking for. I'm not just a country hick, Mr. Hagen. I do have some brains! Whatever you think you've found at Makawsa, you'll find it again somewhere else. Monday morning, bright and early, you are leaving, Mr. Hagen." She slammed the waffle iron down on the counter. "Make your own damn waffles!" She stormed out of the kitchen.

Her heart didn't slow down even when she reached the field below the barn, where Katie was sitting on Mabel's back. "Where's Matt?" Katie called.

"Eating his porridge hot," Annie muttered. "Where's Hortense?" The goat was off his long lead again, and she looked around for him.

"Up there." Katie pointed. Annie turned to see the billy goat feasting on her flowers.

"Oh, blast!" She ran up the hill and tried to shoo him out of her garden. "Get out of here! Go attack the garbage, the way you're supposed to, and leave my flowers alone!" He lowered his head to charge. Katie's laughter pealed out from below as Annie jumped to one side and Hortense rushed by, his bell clanging at his neck. "One more time, Hortense," Annie snarled, "and I swear I'll trade you in for a dog!"

Hortense stopped and looked back over his shoulder at her while chewing in a ruminative manner. Annie pulled a few sprigs of sweet alyssum and held them out to him as a peace offering. "Just stay away from my bachelor's buttons," she told him, scratching him behind the ears as she reattached the lead rope.

She headed for her woodworking tools in the small shop set up in the back of the barn, which she kept locked for safety's sake. After jigsawing twelve elephant puzzles, she shut down the machine and went to check on Katie again.

Matt was sprawled on the grassy slope, propped up on one elbow, listening to Katie as she swung on her tire swing. When she saw her mother, she ran up the hill. "Can I have some cookies, Mommy? I'm starving."

"Two and no more, honey," Annie said. "If you're still hungry, have an apple." She was aware that Matt was walking up the hill toward them. "What were you and Mr. Hagen talking about?"

"Oh, nothing," Katie said innocently and ran for the house. Watching her go, Annie wondered what "nothing" meant.

"I hear you had a little goat trouble this morning," Matt said.

Annie was faintly relieved, hoping that was all Katie had talked about and that she hadn't revealed more family secrets. "Nothing unusual. Hortense has a penchant for my flowers. He's never been overly fond of fresh vegetables."

"What kid is?"

Annie grimaced. "Oh, that's really bad," she said,

laughing in spite of herself.

"It was worth the embarrassment to see you laugh." He admired her openly. "I finished my waffles, by the way. They weren't bad."

"I'm sorry." She was dismayed by her earlier behavior. She should have let his remarks slide, instead of taking them seriously.

"Why? Seems to me that where you're concerned, I have all the finesse of Hortense."

She laughed. "Well, that may be true," she agreed. She nodded toward the river. "Sure you're not interested in fishing? If you need equipment, I have some."

"I did my fishing up on the Smith. Why don't we sit down under that apple tree and talk?" He looked squarely at her in warm, challenging invitation. "Katie should be out again in a few minutes, if you'd feel safer with a chaperone."

"That didn't stop you on the beach yesterday," she told him bluntly.

"There were extenuating circumstances."

"Such as?" she drawled sardonically, her heart racing.

"How were you in chemistry, Annie?"

"Not very good."

"Ah, the drawbridge has just been pulled up, and the princess is locking the door to the tower." His teasing, comprehending smile made her body flush with warmth.

Just then, the screen door slammed, and Katie ran down the hill toward them. Annie noticed she had two big fistfuls instead of just two cookies. "I brought some for Matt," she announced, handing over a whole pile to him. "You're going to love Mommy's cookies, Matt. She's a super cook, 'cept she can't barbecue. But you can do that. She'll make you a big roast tonight with lots of mashed potatoes. Her gravy doesn't have one lump in it. Suzanne says her mother's always looks like brown, watered-down cottage cheese. *Yuk!*"

Annie wondered whether Katie thought the way to Matt Hagen's heart was through his stomach. "Have you fed Prince Charming?"

"He's not awake yet." Katie shrugged.

"There are still the hens," Annie reminded her gently.

As Katie headed for the chicken pen, Annie looked up at Matt, searching for words. He winked at her. "Don't worry about it, Annie."

"I *am* worried," she admitted softly. "She usually doesn't take to people the way she's taken to you."

"It's mutual. She's a little doll."

"That's not the point."

"I know. Monday morning, bright and early, you're evicting me, right? That doesn't mean I won't come back," he told her. "I have a custom van, remember. I can always camp at the head of your road."

"I suppose I should be flattered."

"Instead, you're ready to run for the hills."

"Not quite. I can hold the pass if I have to," she said, vexed.

His eyes shone. "In that case, darlin', you'd better

87

lay in plenty of ammo."

"Mom!" Katie called. "Let's take Matt down to the river."

"Maybe he has something else in mind," she called back, hoping he would drive off somewhere to look over the countryside. When she looked at him again, she caught a sensual glint in his blue eyes. Her mouth tightened. "Fort Ross isn't too far from here. Why don't you go have a look?"

"I've seen it before."

"The Kruse Rhododendron Park, then."

"Take me when the flowers are blooming. We'll spread out a blanket, have some good wine, share a loaf of San Francisco sourdough bread, and . . ." He left the sentence hanging, then laughed at her expression. "Come on, Annie, talk to me." He nodded toward the apple tree.

Katie stayed close to Matt. Annie kept her distance, though she did go down the hill with them. Katie cajoled them into walking down to the Gualala. Annie sat on a grassy bank above the river and watched Matt skip rocks across the water with her daughter. He laughed easily, obviously enjoying Katie's antics and exuberant chatter. Annie found herself daydreaming about what it would be like to be married to him. Would it last? Or would he get tired of being tied down and be on his way again? And why was she even thinking about it?

She remembered what he'd said at the beach about people being like hermit crabs and needing to stay home. It certainly wasn't true of him. Or had he only meant that everyone had a natural element, his being wanderlust and freedom?

Watching him, she thought how devastatingly masculine he was. How many other women on the road had been bowled over by his virile attractiveness, his sexy blue eyes, gravelly voice, and masculine self-confidence? He wanted her—with no subtlety, no subterfuge, but a certain streak of honor, if last night was any indication.

Her own body hummed with desire as she studied him, but she had more than enough reason to draw the line and keep her defenses up. Who was Matt Hagen? *What* was he? Knowing instinctively what it would be like to let him make love to her was all the more reason to keep him at a distance. Sex could be wonderful, miraculous, but it took more to cement a meaningful relationship between a man and a woman than being good in bed together.

Still, it was hard to think about all that when Matt Hagen looked at her.

She closed her eyes and thought about Brent. Remembering him was sure to make her doubly cautious. He was handsome, virile, charismatic. The first time she had seen him, he had been speaking at a political rally for disarmament at Berkeley outside of Sproul Hall. He had made her heart pound and her breath catch, and when he noticed her and seemed to be speaking straight to her, she had immediately fallen in love with him. He had believed in so many things she did—a nuclear bomb free world, civil rights, the ERA. Their courtship had been a mingling of passion, both physical and ideological.

Had she or the world failed him?

For the first two years of their marriage his passion and fiery words had been enough. Then, slowly, she'd begun to see that the words didn't go very deep for Brent. His beliefs were superficial at best. He no longer wanted to be a public defender to help the poor. "There's real money in corporate and tax law, Annie," he'd said. But she hadn't cared about the money.

The doctor had advised her to stop taking birth control pills because of the intense migraines she was suffering, but Brent had been incensed. "Can't you have him prescribe something for the headaches? Just another year or two, Annie. What if you got pregnant? It'd ruin everything."

"He said I'm a candidate for a stroke. Brent. Doesn't that matter to you?"

"Of course it matters, but he's an alarmist. Look at the odds."

She had taken the doctor's advice and also full responsibility for preventing pregnancy. Brent had finished law school cum laude.

Several positions had been offered to him. One was with the superior court as a public defender. Another was with a well-known corporate and tax law firm in San Francisco. Brent had opted for the second.

"You can wait to go back to school, can't you, Annie? There's a house on the bay in Sausalito I want to buy. It's perfect for entertaining. The senior partner told me about it—practically an executive order."

They'd moved from the small inner-city apartment in Berkeley that Annie had worked for months to fix up and established themselves in the modern tri-level in Sausalito.

"There's a right way to decorate and a wrong way," Brent had told her. "We're going to hire a professional."

"No one is going to come into my home and tell me where to put the furniture and what knickknacks to buy!" she'd argued.

"I can't have people coming here with the place looking like an artist's studio. For godsake, Annie, every picture in the house is a watercolor of a dilapidated barn or gristmill, a field with an old broken down fence, or some ragbag kid. If you want paintings of children, buy a Keene. At least it's worth something."

"Only if you plan on selling it!"

He had even begun to disdain her style of dress, wanting her to wear silk dresses at home and Chanel suits when coming to the city. His first case had involved a millionaire charged with tax fraud. Brent had won. The law firm had thrown a big party at the Mark Hopkins Hotel to celebrate. Annie had tried to fit in; she'd tried to make the marriage work; but inside she'd felt her own ideals and principles being crushed.

The crowning blow to their disintegrating marriage

had come when Brent received a lucrative offer to join a law firm in New York City at the same time that Annie found out she was pregnant with Katie.

Opening her eyes, Annie looked down at her little girl, dressed in worn coveralls and tennis shoes, her ponytail swinging as she pitched another rock across the water in a race against Matt Hagen's.

Maybe she should have tried for an amicable divorce. At the time, her anger, hurt, and deep disillusionment had obliterated practicality. Irreconcilable difference had been a gross understatement. She hadn't even asked for alimony, and she hadn't been given it. After all, Brent was an attorney. Everything had been divided equally between them. Brent hadn't honored the child support granted by the court once he'd left California, nor had she pursued her rights in that matter. Maybe that was her biggest mistake.

Katie was going to need braces soon. She longed for a two-wheel bicycle and a trip to the aquarium and Fisherman's Wharf. She's never yet seen a real circus. So many things that mattered so much to a child— things Annie could never seem to afford.

Brent had called her a hippie once, using the term in the most insulting manner. She'd told him simply that, if being a hippie meant living true to one's beliefs rather than selling out, then she was one. It was the only time a man had ever slapped her, and it was the last time she'd seen him other than on opposite sides of a lawyer's conference table.

Annie could hear Katie talking faintly. "Mom was

so mad she said she was going to trade him in for a dog! She won't, though, 'cause she likes Hortense even more than I do. She played matador with him once. She was so funny with that red scarf. She just gets mad at him when he eats her flowers. I wouldn't mind having a dog, but I'd much rather have a parakeet. Suzanne has a parakeet, but I'd know better than to let it stand on my head."

Matt laughed, a natural, amused revelry that appealed to Annie. She watched him skipping rocks with Katie and thought, here is a man who isn't afraid to allow the child in him to come out and play.

She reminded herself yet again that he was leaving Monday morning, and she'd never see him again.

6

MATT ATE A sandwich for lunch while working on his van, and Katie went back down the hill to her swing. Annie managed to pack up the mini-wreath order to deliver during the week. She went to Matt's room to make the bed and found it already made. She freshened the flowers, pulling out the yellow rose to smell it for a moment before putting it back in. She changed his towels and vacuumed, though everything seemed clean. Then she went to the kitchen to begin dinner. Matt Hagen was going to get his chateaubriand.

An hour later, Annie went outside and found Katie

sitting on the porch steps talking to Matt, who had his head buried in the engine of his van. She left them alone again and went to the small workshop in the barn to finish her jigsawing.

She called Katie in for an early bath, just to make sure Matt would have plenty of hot water should he want it. From the look of his hands and forearms, he was going to need it.

"Dinner will be ready at six, Mr. Hagen," she told him from the porch.

"I'll be there," he said, grinning back over his shoulder in a taunting way.

Her heart thumped crazily as she went back inside.

While Annie put the garnish around the carved chateaubriand, Katie set the table in the small, country-style dining room. When Annie carried in the big platter with the meat and vegetables, she found Matt, clean and dressed impeccably in a red shirt and tailored gray slacks, bending over the table to light two white candles Katie had found in the hutch. She had arranged them ingeniously in two small mason jars overflowing with flowers.

"The table looks wonderful, Katie." Annie smiled proudly, setting the platter down. "Come and sit down, honey."

"Are you ready, Matt?" Katie asked excitedly.

"All set." He winked, shaking out the match and giving Annie a devilish glance.

Katie shut off the lights and bounded for her chair before Annie could issue a protest. Matt pushed in her chair and came around the table. "A nice romantic dinner," he said, seating her.

She looked angrily up at him. "Bringing in the Allies?"

He leaned down. "Why not? The siege hasn't even started yet, and you're already in full retreat." He straightened and put his hand lightly on her shoulder, making her muscles tense. He squeezed lightly and let her go before taking his own place at the opposite end of the table.

"I hope you won't object, but we pray before our meal," Annie told him.

"I'm not an atheist," he said simply.

They had hardly begun to eat when Katie asked, "Matt, are you married?"

Annie rolled her eyes heavenward. "Katie!" She shook her head.

Matt chuckled. "No, Katie, I'm not married." He cast an amused look at Annie, who was sitting silently, embarrassed and exasperated. His expression grew serious. "I was married once, but I'm not anymore."

Katie lifted her chin and beamed. "Oh, *good.*"

Annie put her hand over her eyes and wondered whether to take her daughter in the other room for a quick lecture or to just pray she'd hold her tongue for the rest of the dinner.

"Mom's not married either, you know."

"I know," Matt said, his mouth twitching.

"Katie," Annie breathed, "eat. *Now!*" Perhaps, if her mouth was full, she couldn't talk so much.

"Do I have to eat the carrots?"

"No dessert if you don't. You know the rules."

"Mr. Menninger didn't eat *his* carrots, and you gave him dessert," Katie reasoned, referring to a previous guest who'd come with his wife to enjoy the salmon fishing.

Annie gave Katie a straight look. Katie stabbed a carrot, dipped it into some mashed potatoes, and chewed it with a grimace. She gulped down some milk. Eyeing the remaining small pile of carrots on her plate, she said, "What *is* dessert?"

Matt was laughing under his breath at the other end of the table.

Blessed silence reigned for a few moments before Katie launched into a discussion of Suzanne's travels and menagerie of pets. "Matt's been all the way to Disney World, Mommy. Haven't you, Matt?"

With a cunning born of desperation, Annie seized on that subject and milked it through the rest of the meal. She sent Katie to get ready for bed while she began stacking dishes.

"I'll wash, you dry," Matt said.

She glanced back in surprise as he followed her through the, swinging door into the warm kitchen. "Oh, no," she muttered.

He set the platter down on the counter and took her stack of dishes, then turned toward the sink, his arm brushing hers. She edged away. "I can handle things," she said firmly, hoping he'd take the hint and leave.

He didn't. "Good." He moved close again, one hand blocking her retreat toward the refrigerator, the other going behind her as he leaned forward. She drew back as far as she could, her heart pounding. His eyes never left hers. She felt something soft draped over her shoulder. A wary glance identified the dish towel. Matt drew back only a few inches, holding each end of the towel, which he had looped around the back of her neck. "Make a choice, Annie."

"Wash," she said with a dry gulp.

His eyes sparkled with amusement as he slid the towel from around her neck in a suggestive rub. "If I get fresh, are you going to hit me with a wet rag?"

She cleared her throat and tried to step around him. He didn't move. She looked up at him, wondering whether her face was as red as it felt, and if he could hear her heart crashing against her ribs.

"Were you really all that interested in Disney World, or were you trying to divert Katie from her matchmaking efforts?" he asked.

Now she knew her face was as red as it felt! "I'm sorry if she embarrassed you."

His laughing gaze caressed her face tenderly. "You were the one squirming, not me."

"She doesn't really mean anything by it."

"Oh, yes, she does." It didn't seem to worry him at all.

She tilted her chin defiantly. "What if I tell you she brings up the subject with every male over the age of twenty-one?"

"You won't. You said last night she doesn't usually take to people."

"Well, don't let it go to your head," she retorted, and brushed quickly past him. She turned on the taps and squirted liquid detergent into the hot water.

Matt leaned on his elbow on the counter and watched her. She kept her eyes straight ahead as she began washing glasses. He straightened and took the first one from her as she finished rinsing it. "She's pretty impressed with this Suzanne, isn't she?"

Annie sighed. "Yes. The Kintricks take their children someplace every few weeks. This past weekend it was to San Francisco. They went through the aquarium, had tea at the Japanese Gardens, and went for a bay cruise—you name it." She finished another glass. "Last month they went to the circus."

"And Suzanne has a parakeet," he reminded her, laughing softly.

Annie laughed with him. "Yes, I know you heard all about that. Her mother, Marsha, is getting tired of washing Suzanne's hair."

Matt gave her an enigmatic look. "Were you competing with Suzanne's parents when you bought her the cow and goat?" He set the dried glass in the proper cabinet.

She smiled. "Actually, I was fulfilling one of my own fantasies," she admitted, handing him a rinsed plate. "My mother never allowed me to have a pet, and I swore to myself that when I grew up and had children, I was going to let them have as many as they wanted."

"Why didn't you enlist your father's help in getting a pet?" he teased. "Daughters can usually tie their fathers around their little fingers."

She lowered her head and worked on another plate. "My father left us when I was about Katie's age." She turned on the hot water again and rinsed the plate shakily. "I did have a practical reason for choosing a cow and goat," she added, changing the subject abruptly. "I thought Mabel would give us milk, and the man who sold us Hortense swore he ate garbage. The chickens were a gift from a neighbor—Prince Charming and Snow White to start. The others came along later." She knew she was rambling.

Matt's warm hand covered hers as he took the plate. "Do you ever see your father, Annie?"

She tensed. "No."

"Do you know where he is?"

She gave him a resentful glare. "No." She looked away again and reached for another plate. It slipped from her fingers and smashed on the floor. "Oh, damn!" she said miserably.

"Here, let me." Urging her aside, Matt squatted down to collect the broken china. "Was your husband like your father in any way?" he asked, glancing up at her.

She stiffened angrily. "If you want to get so personal, why don't we discuss what caused your divorce, instead of going into mine!"

He straightened slowly. "Where's your trash, Annie? Let's dump this stuff."

She bent and yanked open the cabinet under the sink. He dropped in the glass fragments and nudged the door shut with his knee. Annie turned and began washing dishes again, defensive, but Matt didn't move back out of her way.

"In California vernacular, my wife and I found we didn't relate to each other anymore."

"Whatever that means," she muttered, glaring up at him. "I need some space."

He offered scant inches. "It means that in the beginning we were both afflicted with the same insatiable desires. You keep handing things to me like that, Annie, and you're going to lose another dish."

"I don't want to know *anything* about your insatiable desires, Mr. Hagen."

"They're not the same ones working with us."

"Now, look!"

"It was a bad case of the 'I wants.' A lot of people have it nowadays—it's highly contagious. Katie has a touch of the disease right now. It's a corruption of the American Dream. You can have anything if you're willing to work hard for it. But the more you get, the more you want. And then what you have you've got to keep, even if it means giving up more important things in the process. It's deadly. I wanted to break the fever."

"So you bought a van and bummed around the country."

His eyes grew enigmatic. "The split came well before that," he told her.

She looked down into the sink to avoid his disturbing blue eyes. She could feel him watching her as she scrubbed the flatware, rinsed it, and slid it into the rack. She plopped the baking dish and two pots into the soapy hot water.

"I think you and I believe in the same things, Annie."

She slammed a clean, rinsed pot into the rack. "You don't know anything about what I believe."

"A VIP tax lawyer in New York City, and you here in Gualala raising your little girl and growing your own vegetables—"

"One last time," she enunciated with soft, tight clarity. "I do not want to get involved with you."

His mouth curved faintly. "I know, but for all the wrong reasons."

They stood face to face: Matt clear-eyed, hiding none of his desire; Annie frightened by this man's determination to get into her life.

"You're leaving, so what's the point?" she challenged huskily.

"I'm coming back."

"Matt, please, I really don't need this," she said tremulously, wanting his seduction to stop.

He set the towel aside. "That's where you're wrong, Annie. Everybody on God's green earth needs this. That's why I'm not going to let it slide or allow you to—"

"You're going too fast."

"Maybe," he conceded. "A man can't change completely." He lifted his warm, strong hand to the soft curve of her neck. Her pulse skyrocketed. "You don't have to worry about anything, Annie."

"Oh yes, I do," she said, trembling. How in the name of heaven was she going to keep her head until Monday morning? She stepped back.

Matt studied her face, his expression gently mocking. "You're letting physical attraction stand in the way of our getting to know each other. It shouldn't."

"Unless that's all there is."

"Give yourself a chance to find out. Pretend I'm just your average Joe Blow come to fish the Gualala."

"Just what business were you in?" she asked derisively.

He laughed. "Several."

The kitchen door swung open, and Katie stood there in her pajamas, holding *Charlotte's Web.* "Are you ready to read to me, Mommy?"

Matt winked. "Retreat," he whispered, an amused, all too knowing look in his eyes.

Chapter read and Katie tucked in for the night, Annie decided to let the work on her crafts wait for a while. She glanced toward the living room, where the fire crackled and Matt sat, and told herself she was crazy to feel drawn there. All the while she had read to Katie, she had been overly aware of him sitting relaxed on the couch opposite them, studying her.

But she liked to relax in the living room. Just because he was in there didn't mean she had to hide out in her workroom.

Entering, she looked at him. "Would you like some coffee?" She hadn't meant it to sound like a challenge.

"Why don't we make it brandy?" he suggested. "It might relax us a little bit."

"If you'd prefer," she said, and crossed to the trolley to pour him a large measure of Korbel.

"None for yourself?"

"I don't drink." Lord, she sounded like such a prude. She sank down in the brown corduroy-covered easy chair in which she'd read to Katie and glanced uneasily at him. He was looking straight at her. Her body thrilled softly to that look. He smiled slightly and sipped his brandy, and she let her breath out slowly in a conscious effort to calm down.

"Did you do all this yourself?" he asked, indicating the redwood beams of the living room and the rock fireplace and mantle on which she had set a big, hammered-tin pot with forest greens neatly arranged in it.

"Late-garage-sale," she said, not embarrassed. She had made the rust-gold swag and trim-fitted cascade curtains and added the imitation Nottingham lace sheer curtains from a mail order catalog. The polished wood floor was partly covered by a large rag-weave area rug she'd begun making from cloth remnants when she was first married to Brent. She had bought bags of men's ties from a thrift store to finish it. When they'd moved to Sausalito, Brent had wanted to throw it away, but she'd stored it in the attic along with the two mahogany pedestal tables and Tiffany-style lamps that had been given to her by the octogenarian who had been their Oakland neighbor. The gifts had been in thanks for Annie's doing wash and taking the old woman shopping during the three years they had lived next door.

The couch Matt was sitting on had come from the Salvation Army. She had covered it with tan striped olefin that had come from pieces of two inexpensive throw covers she'd ordered through Sears. One salmon-fishing guest had said his wife had bought a very expensive couch from Ethan Allen that looked exactly like it.

Annie had brightened her living room with quilted, lace-trimmed pillows in yellow, avocado, rust, and chestnut worked in the Mexican Star, Queen Charlotte's Crown, prickly pear, and Nova patterns. She had found the designs in an old quilting book she'd bought from a junk shop along with the coffee table she had refinished. Her own watercolors hung on the walls—all the ones that Brent had once admired and later scorned. Her ficus, philodendron, and four Boston ferns were richly healthy.

"You have a nice touch," Matt said.

"One does one's best with what one has."

"Don't apologize."

"Oh, I'm not," she said truthfully. "Everything is exactly the way I want it. *Everything.*"

He caught her message. His eyes lightened. She was the one to look away first. "What made you pick Makawsa, Annie?"

She relented. Why not admit she wanted to talk with

him, to get to know him, to relish this exciting, rich feeling inside her? Sighing softly, she leaned back in her chair. "Because it was so far away from everything."

"What 'everything' do you mean?"

"Five o'clock traffic, smog, people rushing around all the time, shopping in a supermarket that's bigger than a bowling alley, and never seeing a familiar face. I don't really know . . ." She shook her head. Raising her eyes, she looked straight into his. Why not tell him? "Other things, too. Wearing clothes that were fashionable, but not me. Pouring martinis for people I loathed. Keeping up with the Joneses when I didn't even like the Joneses."

Matt's eyes glowed.

"As you said, my husband and I found we just didn't relate to one another anymore," she said with forced lightness.

His expression softened. "And that hurt."

"Like Hades," she said softly, and glanced away.

"So you bought Makawsa."

"Maybe I went too far. It is rather far from the world."

"But that doesn't bother you."

"No, I love it. But sometimes it's a lonely place for a child."

"You need to add a dog and cat to your menagerie," he teased.

She laughed softly. "I've thought about it, believe me. Maybe I will. Why not?"

The warmth in his blue eyes filled her with physical yearning. She leaned her head back and closed her eyes, trying to shut him out. But she quickly discovered that imagination can be an even headier aphrodisiac. Opening her eyes, she wondered if he could see how she was feeling.

The muscles in his jaw were taut and his eyes were dark. He *knew*. The silence that grew between them wasn't uncomfortable, but it pulsed with more than she was ready to acknowledge.

"I'd better go to bed," she said, standing up. He stood up as well and put down his brandy snifter. Her heart thudded in her chest. "Good night, Mr. Hagen," she said, and headed for the hallway.

"Annie?"

She stopped, her hands clenched at her sides, knowing that if he touched her now, she'd be lost.

He remained where he was. "May I use your telephone? I'll reverse the charges."

She let out her breath. "That would be fine, yes. It's in the hall."

"One more thing."

She waited, looking at him.

He gave her a devastating, crooked smile. "If you can't bring yourself to call me Matt, try Matthew. Please."

7

ANNIE WAS UP well before Matt the next morning, though she'd had difficulty sleeping the night before. She and Katie breakfasted together.

"You'd better get dressed for church, honey," she said, clearing their dishes from the small, intimate kitchen table.

"Is Matt coming with us?"

"He's sleeping."

"Why can't we wake him up and ask him?"

"No. We'll probably be back before he's up."

Later, dressed in their best clothes, they walked up the hill to the small meadow overlooking the river. Annie read verses from her Bible. They sang "Nearer My God to Thee" and "Jesus Loves Me" because they were Katie's favorites.

Once, Annie looked up and saw Matt leaning against a redwood tree, watching them. Her heart leaped. He was wearing snug, worn jeans and a Pendleton shirt with a white T-shirt underneath. Annie raised her hand in greeting. "You're welcome to join us if you like."

He walked toward them, then glanced around at the blue, cloudless sky, the redwoods and alders, the soft ankle-deep grass and scattered wild flowers. "I like your church."

"The architect is nondenominational."

He sat down with them, crossing his legs Indian fashion. "Where were we in the services?"

"We're trying to think of something to do for God this week," Katie told him. She looked at Annie. "How 'bout taking vegetables to Mrs. Richey?" she suggested, referring to an elderly lady down the road who suffered from arthritis.

"We do that already, honey. What about Mr. Roskowick?"

Katie grimaced. "I don't like him. He's *mean*." She looked at Matt. "He has 'No Trespassing' signs all over the place, and he raises rabbits. *To eat!* He's worse than Mr. McGregor in *Peter Rabbit*!"

"That bad," Matt said seriously.

"He's all by himself, Katie."

"He never smiles," Katie insisted. "He always looks like this." She made a forbidding frown and squinted her eyes angrily.

"His wife died of cancer two months ago. Maybe he's crying inside. She was sick for a very long time. You remember her."

"She was nice."

"If she was nice," Matt said softly, "then he can't be all bad, can he, or she wouldn't have stayed with him."

Katie had to ponder that thought. "Okay," she said with a sigh. "We can take Mr. Roskowick some vegetables, too. But you give them to him."

"He has his own vegetable garden," Annie reminded her. "What else could we do for him?"

Katie's eyes brightened. "We could bake him zucchini bread."

Annie smiled. "Okay, we'll do that." They bowed their heads and said prayers for the people Annie and Katie had heard needed them, after which they said thanks for the good things that had happened all week. "Thank you for sending Matt," Katie finished irrepressibly, and jumped up. "Now can I go play?"

"After you go down to the house and change your clothes."

Katie raced down the trail. Matt stood up, and Annie's pulse surged as she looked up at him—big, masculine, his attention focused entirely on her. He held out his hand to help her up. She hesitated, cautious, and then slid her hand into his. When she was standing, she drew back, and he let her go. She smiled up at him more easily.

"Do you have anything planned for today?" he asked as they walked down the hill toward the farmhouse.

"Just puttering."

"Good. Then there's nothing to stop you from spending the whole day with me."

She tried to think of something fast and couldn't. "There's Katie," she said.

"Katie's included."

"What did you have in mind?" she asked warily.

"Something special. *Time.*"

"Can we keep things light?"

"I hope not," he said seriously and chuckled at her

expression. "Come on, Annie. Ease up a little."

"More vernacular, *Matthew?*" He laughed. "Did you fix yourself breakfast already, or do I get the honors this morning?" she asked, smiling.

"I'm starving."

As it turned out, he had to take over cooking his own fried eggs and bacon because the telephone rang. Minnie Wicket lived even farther out of Gualala than Makawsa, and Annie didn't have the heart to cut her off. When she finally hung up after talking at length with Minnie about her son in the marines, Matt was leaning against the arched doorway, smiling.

"I'm sorry," Annie said.

"I managed on my own. Again. Some service you give around here."

"I'm not going to fall into that trap," she told him, seeing the teasing, sensual glint in his eyes. He straightened, and her heart jumped.

The telephone rang again, and she snatched it up. Perhaps it was Minnie again.

Instead, it was a man with a deep, brisk voice demanding Matt Hagen. She raised her brows and held the receiver out to him.

His whole demeanor changed as he took it. She'd seen that expression on Brent's face hundreds of times before. *Business.*

"Matt Hagen here." Annie went down the hall. "Who gave you this number?" he demanded. "The answer's no. Tough. That was sixteen months ago. Things have changed. I said no." He laughed harshly.

"Go ahead if you think it'll do you any good."

Annie closed her bedroom door. Whoever was on the other end of that telephone line was getting an ear blistered. She changed into faded blue jeans and an embroidered yellow tunic which she belted with a long strip of multi-colored cloth she wound around her waist twice and tied in a square knot. When she came out, Matt was still on the phone.

"I don't care what he offered. You know what he'd do when he got in there," he snapped. His feet were planted apart, and his free hand was propped on his hip in a stance of angry impatience. "Look, we'll discuss all this when I get back and not before. I said no. That stands. No, I'm not coming back tonight." He gave an abrupt, humorless laugh. "Maybe. I haven't decided yet. You've handled things this long, what's a few more days?"

Annie passed him quietly and headed for the front door. Matt glanced around sharply. "It's in Mexico!" he said sharply and hung up. "Annie, wait a minute."

She'd opened the door to go out. Looking back at him, she felt the sizzling aura of restrained nervous tension and excitement emanating from him. As he walked toward her, her body tensed. He put his hand up and pushed the door shut with a bang. The telephone rang again; his expression tightened as he cast it a glowering look. She ducked under his arm and went back to answer it, thankful for the timely interruption.

"Where's Gualala?" came a different man's voice from the first who'd called.

"Pardon me? Gualala is—"

Matt reached her in two steps and snatched the telephone from her. "Call again and our deal's off!" He slammed down the receiver.

Annie stared up at him, her heart thundering.

"I'd forgotten what it was like," he said cryptically, giving her a rueful look. She turned toward the door. He followed, reaching around to open it for her.

Katie was down the hill swinging. She jumped off and ran toward them. "Can we go back up in the woods again?"

"If your mom will come along," he said, glancing at Annie. She nodded.

They all walked up toward the alders and ferns behind the farmhouse. There was a narrow trail along which Katie raced with the agility of a fawn, leaping over tree roots. She called back to them, "I'm going to the elf's ears!"

"The *what?*" Matt said.

"Pink fungus on the fallen tree," Annie translated. "It looks like ears."

The smell of damp earth, fern, and pine was heady. Several birds burst from a bush just above them and winged up through the branches. Katie laughed, racing on and climbing up onto the huge, fallen redwood up the hill. "King of the Mountain! King of the Mountain!" Her singsong child's voice echoed through the forest before she jumped off on the other side.

Annie could feel Matt close behind her. Katie was

well ahead, and she had the desire to run and put some distance between herself and the man following her. She reached the fallen redwood.

Matt stepped ahead and swung himself across so he could reach back to help her. He caught hold of her at the waist and lifted her down. She held her breath, looking up at him. His hands still gripped her firmly. They loosened and moved up against her ribs. She caught hold of his forearms and shook her head.

"Annie . . ." he whispered huskily, his eyes darkening.

"We'd better keep going."

"She's not going to leave us far behind." His fingers spread against her. Another half inch and his thumbs would be lightly brushing against the undersides of her breasts, which felt heavy and tingly with anticipation. She saw the muscle in his jaw tighten. His eyelids lowered slightly as he looked down at her mouth.

She tried to step back, but his hands tightened in silent protest. She put hers more firmly against his biceps and felt the incredible strength he had. "Matt, please, don't . . ." she managed to say breathlessly.

"I can't stop remembering what's it like to kiss you."

"Try harder."

"How can you be rational when we feel like this?"

"The instinct of preservation. Now let go, please."

He searched her eyes, then did as she asked. She stepped quickly around him and hurried to the top of the trail. With trembling fingers, she combed back the damp strands of hair from her flushed cheeks and glanced back at Matt who was coming more slowly. He gazed up at her, his eyes faintly mocking.

Katie was skipping through the grass in the meadow. They called this their *"Sound of Music"* hill. But instead of an Austrian village and the Alps beyond, there stretched the wide, blue Pacific. Annie could smell it faintly in the soft breeze that stroked her face.

"Guess what I've got?" Katie called, and she held up a big orange she had pilfered from the fruit bowl before leaving the house. Her urchin face split into a mischievous grin. "If you want some, you have to catch me!"

"You head her off that way," Matt instructed in a laughing undertone. Annie laughed, too, and started stalking her daughter. Katie squealed in delight and raced across the meadow, her pigtails flying. She ducked into the trees. Matt plowed in after her. He emerged a few minutes later, laughing. "Where'd the little dickens go?"

"Yoo-hoo!" Katie called, and they spotted her perched ten feet up in a pine tree.

"You little monkey. Come down from there!" Annie called.

"Matt, you looked so silly hunting around in the bushes," Katie giggled, coming down. The orange bulged from the inside of her T-shirt.

They sat in the sun and shared the snack. Then Katie was off again, hunting for treasures to fill her pockets. Matt stretched out on his side, his head propped up on his hand, just looking at Annie, who sat cross-legged in the grass. Katie came running up and dumped a handful of flowers in her lap. "For you, Mommy," she said breathlessly before racing off again.

Matt chuckled, watching her go. "She's something."

Annie smiled. "She'll sleep well tonight." Her smile died abruptly as she realized he might misunderstand.

"Don't worry so much," he teased.

She toyed with the wild flowers, avoiding his gaze.

"Matt, come here!" Katie called.

He levered himself up. "Maybe now you'll relax, hmm?" He winked and walked off. She watched the way his body moved with a lithe, virile grace, and her stomach plunged in desire. Katie came running to meet him and tugged excitedly at his hand.

Annie watched them for a few minutes and then lay flat on her back to look up at the clouds. It was a favorite game of Katie's. "Make a shape of the cloud, Mommy," she'd say. "What's that? A dragon. A bear over there."

But the clouds Annie saw today moved together in a floating undulation. Her imagination wound a man and woman together in passion. She could hear Matt's deep voice telling Katie something about pine nuts and squirrels.

Her lips parted softly on a slow, calming sigh, but her heart still knocked erratically in her breast. She closed her eyes and, unbidden, the stirring memory of Matt kissing her in the workroom returned to her. She remembered the hard contours of his aroused body, his restless tension as his kiss became an urgent possession. Imagination carried the incident further.

"Dozing?" Her eyes flew open. Matt was sitting beside her, his arm braced across her body.

"Where's Katie?" she croaked, blushing hotly at the sound of her husky voice.

His gaze narrowed slightly as he studied her, and a faint smile played on his mouth. "Hmm," he said thoughtfully, taking one of the flowers Katie had strewn across her lap and tucking it behind Annie's right ear. He picked up another and ran it provocatively along her jaw, across her lips, and over her cheek before putting it in her hair. His fingertips lightly brushed her cheek and traveled slowly downward before lifting over the quivering swell of her taut breasts. Somehow, the fact that he didn't touch her there was all the more exciting.

He picked up a wild daisy from her abdomen, his fingertips grazing her and sending tremors into the pit of her stomach. "Did you ever read D. H. Lawrence, Annie?" Her face burned as she recognized his reference. He laughed softly, the light in his eyes accelerating her heartbeat even more. "I can see you did."

She started to push herself up onto her elbows to escape, but he leaned forward, and she realized how close her mouth would be to his. She sank back down.

"It's always been a fantasy of mine to chase my woman through the woods and catch her. We would lie together in a sun-warmed meadow just like this, and I'd decorate her beautiful body with wild flowers before I made—"

"Let me up," she demanded, her voice noticeably trembling.

He leaned back on his hand, giving her just a few inches, and waited. She moved restlessly, edging back, but her hip brushed his. She sat up. He looked straight into her eyes and tucked the daisy into the front of her scoop-neck tunic so that the stem stroked across her hard nipple. She opened her mouth in shock, and he kissed her. It was a brief kiss, but the effect resounded like a drum roll through her body before he drew back and stood up.

He reached down and pulled her to her feet. "Katie's hungry," he said in a low, gravelly voice, "and so am I." His own hunger blazed openly in his eyes.

He didn't touch her again as they walked down the hill, but he didn't need to. Annie felt his presence as if he were a part of herself, and her imagination fueled all the details of what he hadn't finished.

"Need help fixing lunch?" he asked softly when they reached the front steps. His hand rested on the railing near her hip.

If he came inside, they would never get to lunch. She shook her head, making a mute appeal. He raised his hand and took one of the flowers from her hair. "Okay, Annie."

She served lunch on the porch. Katie did most of the talking. Matt watched Annie with amused intensity.

She escaped back into the house as soon as she could.

She was polishing a copper pot when Katie came in. "Matt stacked up all the firewood," she announced, diving into the cookie jar.

"What?"

"He's splitting some, too. Can I have some milk, please?"

"Help yourself, honey," she said, untying her apron and hanging it on the hook before she went outside. She found Matt swinging an ax behind the carport.

"I can split my own wood, Matt," she told him defensively.

He gave her slender, but decidedly curved form a sweeping glance. "Woman's liberation?"

"We've been up here for almost six years, and we've managed."

He leaned on the ax and looked at her solemnly. "I need a way to burn off some energy, Annie. It's either this or chasing you around the woods. Which do you prefer?" She left him to his splitting.

When Matt brought his duffel bag outside the next morning, ready to leave, she followed him. Katie had already left for the bus stop at the head of the driveway, and everything seemed too quiet.

He slid the van door shut with a loud bang. She came down the steps and held out a twenty-dollar bill.

His mouth tightened. "What's that for?"

She gave him a faint, apologetic smile. "I over-charged you."

118

His expression cleared with amusement. He reached out, put it back into her palm, and closed her fingers tightly. "Room deposit for my next visit."

Her throat ached.

"I'll call you. Annie."

But he didn't. Not that day or the next. Or the next.

8

"WHO'S THIS MATT we keep hearing so much about?" Suzanne's mother, Marsha, asked as she and Annie sat on the porch drinking coffee. Katie had spent the afternoon at their house, and Marsha had brought her home.

"Just a guest we had for the weekend," Annie announced evasively, offering her a kislin cookie, a Scandinavian butter cookie.

"Oh, is that all?" Marsha's hazel eyes sparkled merrily in her freckled face. "The way Katie tells it, he was a mixture of Superman and Richard Gere all rolled into one incredible hunk." She laughed.

"He only spent three days here," Annie said, hoping the lasting impression he had left didn't show in her face. Why couldn't she just forget all about Matt Hagen? She'd known what he was the moment she'd laid eyes on him: undependable.

"But he's coming back, right?"

"I doubt it. Greener pastures elsewhere. You know the type."

"That type doesn't chop firewood for you, or help with the dishes."

Annie glanced up sharply. "What else did Katie tell you?"

Marsha sipped her black coffee and munched on her cookie with a bland countenance. Her mouth twitched. "Hmm, not much."

"Come on, Marsha."

"That he had a blue van with a *bed* in it," she said wickedly. "Imagine! And a CB radio and tape deck. Oh, and he put flowers in your hair and promised to come back and fix the barn loft so Katie could play in it. Among other things."

Annie's face burned.

Marsha smiled gently at her. "I've never known you to look twice at a man, so if one managed to put flowers in your hair and kiss you, he had to be something. Who is he?"

"His name is Matt Hagen."

"Hagen." Marsha frowned. "The name sounds familiar. Where is he from?"

"San Francisco, all over. I don't know. What does it matter? He won't be back, and just as well. Believe me."

Marsha looked searchingly at her, then mercifully changed the subject.

That evening Annie tried again to talk to Katie about Matt, but Katie remained convinced that he would be back soon, just as he had said he would. But the next week passed without a word. Katie spoke less of him, and Annie hoped she would soon forget him entirely.

She was elbow-deep in dishwater when the telephone rang. "Honey, will you get that? I'll be right there."

The phone stopped ringing. "It's Matt, Mommy!" Katie cried.

Annie's heart jumped. "Oh, damn!" she muttered, drying her hands. When she came out of the kitchen, Katie was talking with more animation than she had since he'd left.

"When are you going to come back and fix the loft?"

"Kathleen Patricia, let me have that telephone," Annie said quickly. "Hello?"

"Annie," was all he said, and, at the sound of his deep, husky voice, she wasn't sure she could answer. "I'm sorry I didn't call sooner, but—"

"No need to apologize. What can I do for you, Mr. Hagen?" she said in a noncommittal tone.

The pause from the other end of the line was loaded. "How was Mr. Roskowick?" he asked, nonplussing her.

"Mr. Roskowick? He . . . he was fine."

"Was Katie afraid of him?"

"Not after he gave her a baby rabbit," she said, smiling in spite of herself.

Matt chuckled. "The menagerie is growing. How's old Hortense?"

Annie tried not to let his charm get to her. "Why did you call?"

He sighed. "I'm coming up again this weekend."

"There's no room for you at the inn," she lied.

"Then I'll camp at the head of your road."

Just as he had threatened. She looked at Katie standing there, her heart in her eyes, listening. "Honey, go to your room for a few minutes. I'll come to tuck you in as soon as I've finished talking to Matt."

"Awww, Mommy . . ."

"Now, Katie!" She watched her walk glumly down the hall and into her room. Her hand tightened on the receiver. "Don't come back here, Matt," she said firmly, her eyes closed tightly. When he said nothing, she felt compelled to add in a softer voice, "Please, you're only going to hurt her."

"I'm not going to hurt either one of you."

"You already have. I . . . she's been waiting for you to call for *eight* days."

"Annie, I've been working long hours trying to work things out so—"

"You don't owe me explanations, and I don't want any," she said defensively, trying to put the conversation on an impersonal level.

Another silence fell. Then Matt said in a hard tone, "I've got twenty dollars holding that room."

She sucked in her breath. "Give me your address, if you have one, and I'll be more than glad to return your deposit."

"Not a chance. I'll see you before noon on Saturday." He hung up.

Annie's heart didn't slow down for ten minutes.

Her emotions remained in a jumble for the next two days. If she'd known where Matt was and how to reach him, she would have called and asked him again not to come. If one visit had caused this much turmoil in her, how much would *two* visits cause?

Katie, of course, was ecstatic. Annie tried to reason gently with her, to explain that, just because Matt was coming again, it didn't mean he would keep coming back. She mustn't get her hopes up. But her words of warning did no good at all.

By Saturday morning Annie was in a state of high nervous tension. She was planning to have a serious talk with Matt Hagen about the heartache he could cause Katie by encouraging this attachment. But when the blue van pulled up the drive and he got out, she felt sure her heart was permanently lodged in her throat.

She stood at the top of the steps. Katie felt no such restraints and bounced down them to fling herself into his arms. He laughed, hugging her close. "Say! Now, that's the kind of welcome a man likes," he said, lifting her high. "How ya doin', Kitten?"

"Are you going to fix the loft, Matt?" Annie felt her face fill with hot color. Matt set Katie down again and tugged on one of her pigtails. "Mom said you wouldn't come back, but I knew you would."

He looked up at Annie, and her stomach curled into

a tight knot. "I came back, and I'll keep coming back," he said, looking straight at her, no lightness in his tone or look. "There's something in the van for you, Katie. It's unlocked." As she darted around the side and struggled to open the door, he came up the steps toward Annie. He stopped one step below her, bringing them to eye level. "I missed you."

She swallowed. "Your room is ready," she said tonelessly.

He came up the last step. Catching hold of her wrist, he opened the front door and pulled her inside abruptly. "What are you—" she began, the screen door slamming behind them, finding herself pulled into his arms.

Heat exploded in her abdomen as he took her mouth in a hungry, no-holds-barred kiss. She arched back, trying to free herself, but his arms tightened. His hand cupped the back of her head, holding her mouth captive against his to deepen the kiss. After a moment nothing seemed to matter but to kiss him back and let it last for as long as he wanted.

When he released her, he stroked her cheek with a shaking hand. "I needed that, and so did you," he whispered hoarsely.

Reason was coming back. Her eyes burned. She shook her head, her eyes pleading, and moved out of his embrace. "Just . . . just what did you come back to get?" she asked chokingly.

His eyes darkened in anger. "We won't make love until you can handle the situation." Her lips parted in protest. His expression softened. "I want you like hell, Annie, but it doesn't take a genius to know you're scared to death of what you're feeling. I'm not going to rush you into bed, but don't expect me to keep my distance, either. I can't. Dammit, I won't."

What an odd thing to claim when he'd been gone for so long. She didn't dare ask him to explain, knowing how much that question would reveal about her own confusion.

"Mommy! *Mommy!*" Katie was laughing delightedly. "Come see what Matt brought me!"

A smile danced in his eyes as he held the screen door open for her. She stepped quickly through and went back out onto the porch. He followed and leaned against the front pillar, his hands in his front jeans pockets in a pose of casual innocence.

"What is it?" Annie called.

Katie climbed out of the van and reached back inside to bring out an oriental-fashion gilded cage. "Look!"

"Oh, Lord, no," Annie muttered, putting a hand to her forehead. She cast Matt a half-angry, half-laughing look. "A parakeet, by any chance?"

"Lovebirds."

"Birds?" she repeated, alarmed. "How many birds?"

"Only two, but, as with any loving pair, more could come along later." His eyes glinted warmly with a less-than-subtle message.

"Aren't they pretty?" Katie cried, bringing the cage

up to Annie. "Can I keep them in my room? Please? *Please?*"

"They'd be happier in the living room with lots of sunlight, Katie," Matt informed her. "And your mom could enjoy them, too."

"Since I'll be cleaning the cage, that would be nice," Annie said dryly, raising an admonishing brow at him as Katie carried the cage inside. "It was nice of you, but I really wish you hadn't."

"You don't object to the birds. You object to me bringing gifts," he said solemnly.

"Yes. You're only making things harder for Katie in the long run," she said, not dissembling.

"That's going to depend on you, Annie, not me," he said, and went down the steps to get his things from the van.

Katie followed him outside like his shadow. Annie came out to investigate later when she heard pounding in the barn. She found Matt yanking up rotten timbers in the loft. A stack of new lumber lay below him.

She almost choked. "You're not planning to put this up there!"

"Sure am," he told her, tossing down a jagged one-by-eight to clatter on the growing pile at one side.

"But . . . but this is high-grade wood for shelving!"

"What difference does it make?" he asked, hooking the claw end of his hammer beneath another board.

"About a dollar a foot, that's what difference it makes. Just stop what you're doing right now. What

126

gives you the right to rip out my loft in the first place?"

He swung around so that his legs dangled from a rafter. "Katie plays up here, and it isn't safe."

"She's been told not to—"

"Kids will be kids, Annie. You want her to fall through the floor?"

"Of course I don't!"

"Then put away your little mental calculator. This one's on me."

"No, it is not!" She stalked out and went to call the Fort Bragg lumberyard for an estimate of what the materials would cost. Afterward she sat down glumly in the living room, her head in her hands. She wondered vaguely what Matt had been doing for ten days that he had so much money to burn.

They ate dinner in virtual silence. Katie's eyes darted between her mother and Matt in distress. She was uncharacteristically quiet.

Matt didn't try to help with the dishes; instead, he was drafted by Katie to read their latest project, *The Swiss Family Robinson.* Annie worked in the kitchen, her resentment growing, her worry intensifying.

"Why're you so mad at Matt, Mom?" Katie asked when Annie tucked her into bed.

"Just don't worry about it, honey," Annie said, kissing her on the forehead, her heart constricting at the look of concern on daughter's face. "It has nothing to do with you."

Matt was waiting for her at the living room

archway. He had added an oak log to the fire. She looked pointedly from it to him. "That'll burn well past midnight."

"Do you think that's going to be enough time to iron out all of your hang-ups?" he asked quietly.

"No hang-ups," she said with a challenging lift of her chin. "Just a few justifiable concerns and objections."

"Shoot."

She glared at him. "You can't buy me or my daughter."

"I'm not trying to, Annie," he said very calmly.

"No? Then why lovebirds and lumber for the loft?"

"Because I wanted to give you both something you would enjoy, and I've been worried about Katie playing up there and you trying to fix it on your own."

"I'm perfectly capable—"

"No doubt," he said in a tone that raised her hackles.

"I don't want you to bring gifts to us or do any of my repairs," she told him. *"Please."* It came out like a curse.

"You gave fresh-baked zucchini bread to Mr. Roskowick."

"You know it's not the same thing!"

"Why not?" he retorted, walking slowly to where she stood in the middle of the room. Her heart jumped nervously as he came closer. "Because there's a few dollars' difference? What the hell, Annie. If I can afford it, who cares? It's all to the same purpose, isn't it? You wanted to lighten the man's heavy load a little, cheer his day, show him someone cared. Why do you begrudge me the same chance?"

Said in just that way and in just that tone, she felt small for arguing the issue. But other questions kept coming. How could he afford it? What had he been doing for ten days that he could burn a couple of hundred dollars on lovebirds, gilded cages, and lumber, not counting the fifty-five dollars a night to stay at Makawsa? Just what had he done? Robbed a bank?

Yet, if she wanted to put distance between them, she could hardly launch into a barrage of personal questions about how he made his living, *if* he did, and where he had gone when he'd left Makawsa.

"What do you want to know, Annie?" he asked, his mouth curved slightly. "Come on, ask. Your mind is moving faster than BART. Are you wondering where I got the money?"

She blushed. "It's none of my business."

"Your favorite litany," he muttered, impatience briefly shadowing his eyes. "All right. Would it be your business if I were trafficking drugs?"

She blanched. Surely he wasn't serious! "I'd tell you to get out of my house this minute." She searched his face. "You aren't, are you?" she asked faintly, unable to believe it.

"What do your instincts tell you?"

"No," she said frankly.

"And you'd be right, Annie. Two years ago I'd have done a lot of things to make money, but even then I had principles." He took her hand and guided her to

129

the couch near the fire. She looked at him warily as he sat down beside her. She shifted a few inches away. His eyes twinkled.

"Your instincts should have told you a few basic things about me, too," she said stiffly, meaning that he should know she wanted to keep space between them.

He chose to answer the challenge in a different way. "Yes, I think so. I think you filed for divorce and wanted everything split fairly down the middle. You didn't ask for anything, and you didn't get anything. Right? Except perhaps child support, which I'd hazard a guess he never sent."

"How would you know all that? And why bring it up now?"

"Because you work hard for everything you have, and if you were getting a fat check from your wealthy ex-husband and child support for Katie, you'd have things a lot easier. As it is, you spend Katie's school days and your evenings working, right? And Katie still hasn't had her dream trip to the aquarium and Fisherman's Wharf, or seen a circus."

Her mouth tightened defensively. Where was this leading? "All in due time."

"She's getting better stuff, Annie. From you."

She searched his warm eyes. He stretched his arm out behind her. "Now, if I know all that, how could I possibly think you would be a woman I could buy?"

Her heart tripped heavily and her mouth went dry. She clenched her hands tightly in her lap, trying to still the rampant desires flooding her body.

130

"I love the way your eyes go all smoky," he whispered, reaching out to stroke her braid. His hand rested on her shoulder, his thumb brushing small, erotic circles on her skin. Even through the light cotton blouse, the touch of his hand sent heat down into her breasts and made her tremble.

Matt leaned slowly toward her. She put her hand up, spreading it in protest against his hard chest. His heart was racing.

"I want you, Annie," he murmured hoarsely. "You're in my life to stay, whether you're ready or not."

"I don't sleep with my guests, Matt. House rules."

He gave her a tender, understanding look. "I'd hazard another guess," he whispered and lowered his mouth to her temple. "You haven't slept with anyone since your divorce." His lips moved slowly down the curve of her neck, sending thrills of pleasure along her nerve endings.

"Can the same be said for you?" she managed to say thickly.

"No." He drew back slightly to look down at her.

"How many along the road?"

He frowned, something close to regret flickering in his eyes. "Does it matter?"

She bit down on her lower lip, her facial muscles giving a little telltale jerk. "How many were lonely landladies, Matt? One? Six? How many places have you stopped during your sixteen-month odyssey?"

His eyes went dark. "I was looking for answers,

Annie, not a string of willing bed partners. I stopped in a lot of places where there weren't any people at all, least of all women."

"Ah, but there were women, weren't there?" She hated the hurt sarcasm in her tone.

"A few," he conceded. "If I'd known someone like you was at the end of the road, I'd have slept alone."

"Why? These days everyone sleeps with everyone," she said brittlely.

"You don't."

"No, I don't," she said firmly.

"Something else I knew about you by instinct."

"Ah, but you keep trying to change that," she said, grasping his wrist and stopping his hand from its provocative caress.

"Malice aforethought?" he asked dryly.

"I know how it must seem to you," she said. "A divorcée, alone in the woods . . . easy game."

"How?" he bit out.

What could she say to that? Admit that his touch aroused her more than any other man's ever had? Admit that she yearned to know everything about him, past, present, and future? Admit that, even while trying not to, she fantasized about him making love to her? He probably knew that already. Looking into his eyes, she was convinced he did.

"I didn't have to come in here," she admitted with difficulty.

"You almost didn't," he said and sighed heavily. He moved back slightly, giving her a little more room.

"I'm not trying to break your resolve, Annie. I just need to touch you." He let out a soft breath. "Sometimes I think there's a basic sexual impatience built into a man when he finds the woman who's right for him."

Her heart bounded.

Matt ran a stimulating finger along the line of her flushed cheek. "Timidity, too," he murmured huskily, his own vulnerability glimmering in his eyes. "Inevitably, Annie, it's the woman who has the final say as to whether she's willing to take the man on or not."

Her breathing was shallow as his hand moved along the curve of her neck, sending shivers of hot anticipation and liquid desire through her body. She felt the tremor in his fingers, saw the flame burning in his eyes.

"Matt . . ."

His hand moved up again, his fingers curving around the thick French braid at the back of her head and drawing her toward him. She couldn't find her voice, nor her previously mentioned resolve. Her lips parted when he kissed her, and he groaned, his hand tightening. His mouth moved back and forth on hers, his tongue probing the sweet recesses of her mouth.

He pulled her close, bringing her hip against his as he leaned heavily across her, pressing her back against the couch. His hand moved down, cupping her breast, his thumb lightly outlining the aching peak. She gave a soft, ecstatic moan.

Matt drew back, his breathing audible. "Oh, Annie, love, I don't want to blow it with you," he said against her temple.

Unthinking, she lifted her head and sought his mouth again. He kissed her with an urgency that fired her blood. He drew back again, gripping her arms. "Stand up," he whispered hoarsely, doing so and pulling her up with him. He swept her close so that their bodies were pressed together. She could feel the enormity of her effect on him as he took her mouth again. He tilted her head to deepen the fiery kiss, his hands moving down her body, molding her to him. He caught her hips tightly and arched against her. She had to spread her feet to keep from swaying off-balance, which made his movement all the more provocative.

Who was breathing hardest or trembling most? She could feel his heart thundering. His body was hot, tense, hard.

"Oh, Lord," Matt groaned against her hair. "If I lay you back on that couch, it'll be all over but the shouting, Annie," he said thickly. "And you won't be able to look at yourself—or me—in the morning." He moved away from her, and she saw in his face the cost of that effort. He cupped her face with shaking hands and kissed her lightly before letting her go entirely.

"Go to bed, Annie. Now, before I change my mind and take you there," he murmured hoarsely. "I'm going out for a long, cool walk."

She watched him step around her and go out into the hallway. The front door opened and closed. She knew then that she was falling in love with him, and wondered if she was making the second biggest mistake of her life.

9

THE WEATHER WAS cold and overcast the next morning. Annie sat with Katie in the living room for their weekly family worship. They decided to make several dozen cookies, tie up some magazines, and deliver some fresh produce to a convalescent home in Santa Rosa. They would deliver everything while dropping off the completed order of pink elephant puzzles.

Matt sat nearby, listening but saying little. While Annie went to make beds, dust, and see to the general tidying of the house, Katie coerced him into a game of Scrabble.

Donning her pea-coat and watch cap, Annie went out to see to the chickens and animals. Matt followed a few minutes later, hunched into his heavy fatigue jacket. He was hatless, the wind ruffling his dark hair. She scattered feed to the chickens, aware of his gaze on her.

"What's Katie up to?" she asked, his silence making her nervous.

"She's doing a color-by-number."

She glanced at him. "Hmm. Where did she get that?"

He grinned. "Oh, just a little something I brought along to keep her occupied while I pursue her mother."

Annie laughed softly in embarrassment. He was teasing, while at the same time not teasing. She checked the raised wooden boxes for eggs while the hens were pecking feed on the ground. She took off her watch cap and put in six eggs.

Matt opened the gate for her, pushed back an escaping hen with his boot, and latched the gate behind her. "Your ears are getting pink," he observed. "Here, let me put the eggs in my coat pockets and you put your cap back on before you're blue."

She grinned. "Careful," she told him, handing over her take, "or you'll have a real mess on your hands."

He chuckled. "Your jokes are even worse than mine."

"Something we have in common?"

"We have a lot in common," he said seriously, walking with her as she started down the hill toward a grim-looking Hortense.

She paused long enough to pick some flowers from her garden and glanced at Matt. "Such as?"

"We both want to 'get away from it all.'"

"What 'all' did you want to get away from when you left the city?"

His eyes warmed noticeably. "Finally decided to get nosy?"

She shrugged. "Tit for tat."

"Okay. Tension headaches, no time for anything but

business, doing business with jerks, getting audited by the IRS, dealing with fine print, and realizing that at the rate I was going I'd have a heart attack before I was fifty and maybe never even enjoy life. And never having time for important things, like keeping in touch with friends."

Annie watched his face as he talked and saw how taut he was, how his eyes narrowed almost in anger and sparked with an inner sadness.

"What was the final straw, Matt?"

A pained grimace crossed his tanned brow, and he sighed. "The death of a friend," he answered in a flat tone. He frowned heavily, his eyes intent, searching hers. "What was *your* last straw, Annie?"

"My husband's last request," she told him bleakly, her face cold with remembered pain and anger. She turned away and began walking again, her hand clenched around the flowers she had picked for Hortense. She had said it as though Brent had died.

In a way he had. The Brent she had loved and married had died sometime during those six years together. Had it been her fault? When she'd married him, she'd been so sure it would last forever. He was intelligent, fun, and handsome, and those qualities had mattered. So too had his integrity and high ideals. Then the latter two had been eaten away by his ambition and desire for "success." Without the fiber to hold his character together, she found that intelligence, charm, and good looks didn't matter a tinker's damn. Not even when they were employed full strength against her.

The last straw . . .

Her eyes smarted.

"We're treading on hallowed ground, aren't we?" Matt remarked, keeping pace easily, one of his long strides equivalent to one and a half of hers. She slowed down and forced herself to smile up at him.

"As long as we talk in nuances, we'll get along just fine," she said lightly.

He caught her hand, halting her. "Let's cut the nuances. I'm not looking for safe and comfortable. I want to get in deep with you, Annie. Up to my neck. Over my head."

"I bet you'd be hell on wheels in a boardroom or standing in court pleading a case." She freed her hand.

"I'm just trying to ford your damn moat," he said tightly.

She knew that. He was halfway up the stairs to the tower, and she was madly slamming the doors against him. "You're in such a big hurry. You're so relentless."

"We could have made love last night."

Her mouth tightened. "Yes, you're right. Last night, for a bum who travels around the country, you showed amazing character," she retaliated.

His expression cleared, though his eyes were no less dark. He even smiled sardonically. "You think I'm just a bum looking for an easy touch, is that it?"

"I don't know what you are," she said frankly.

"I'd take it as a compliment if you were interested enough to ask."

"But you don't even know," she shot back. "You've been driving all over America looking for yourself!"

He laughed. "Annie, if only you knew. I'm not a bum, believe me."

"You could tell me anything, Matt, but it wouldn't necessarily be the truth." Brent had known where he was going, but he'd ended up someplace else entirely.

Matt looked at her curiously. "What made you so cynical, Annie?"

"Experience." She swung away again, marching toward the goat, who eyed the flowers in her hand. She held them out to him, while glancing back at Matt, who was watching her.

"Weren't you looking for something when you came up here to Makawsa?" he challenged, walking toward her again.

"No. I knew exactly what I wanted up here. Fresh air, space; people who want more from life than grubbing for another buck or stabbing a competitor in the back to make a bigger deal. I wanted to go back to simple things, like having time with my baby, and smelling wild flowers, and wading barefoot in a river . . ."

"And finding solitude in which to lick your wounds."

She let out her breath. "All right, that too," she admitted.

He smiled then, warmly. "Now we're getting down to it."

Why not be honest with him? she thought. Wasn't that her own litany? Be honest! Be honest! Annie let the flowers drop and faced Matt, her hands on her hips. "All right. Nuances aside. It's taken me seven long years to put my life back together and be happy again, Matt. It wasn't easy, and I don't want to go into the details of what happened. Just take my word that I couldn't bear that kind of disillusionment again."

"But that's not all of it."

"No, it isn't. Katie took one look at you and went gaga. She treats you like her long-lost father, and you encourage it. I'm scared. I don't want to hurt her. You don't know where you're going—"

"That's where you're wrong. I know exactly where I'm going."

Her heart jumped, but she pressed on ahead in self-defense. "Oh, you *think* you know, now. You have all the answers, don't you? But you weren't so sure a while back, or you wouldn't have left whatever it was you left because you didn't like it, and gone off to hunt for something you would. Lord, I was married to a man who *knew* what he wanted, then changed." She hadn't meant to blurt that out.

"I want *you,* Annie. *And* Katie."

She bit her lower lip, seeing the look in his eyes and feeling her own response to it. "You're a very attractive man—"

"We said we'd cut the nuances," he told her gruffly.

She took a deep breath. "Yes." She swallowed. "I'm attracted to you, too, but—"

"Something stronger than that, Annie," he said frankly.

She blinked. Letting out a shaky breath, she said, "You remind me of a song Katie learned in kindergarten and sang for weeks on end. It went 'I'm being swallowed by a boa constrictor.' That's exactly how I feel around you. You come here, a complete stranger, and try to swallow me whole. You look at me and kiss me and churn me up inside so I can't think straight, then you're gone again to wherever. For eight days, not one word. Now, here you are back again, picking up where you think you left off. And you'll be gone again tomorrow."

"I suppose it might seem that way to you," he conceded.

"It *is* that way."

"For a little while it has to be."

It was odd how much that hurt.

He came closer. "Annie, when I leave here, I go back to San Francisco to clear up business I left behind."

"For sixteen months? Some business you've got."

"I turned things over to someone else in my absence. Now I've got to make a pack of decisions again. That's what I'm doing: putting my decisions into action." They were lulling words, vague answers to unvoiced questions. What was he really talking about? "I don't want to go into it all," he told her. "It's so damn complicated. I just want to go into us. That's all that's important."

"What *us?*"

"You feel it as well as I do. This kind of feeling just doesn't come along every day. Love, Annie. If you

141

want safety, that's the only place you're ever going to find it. I want to nurture it the way you do your garden: weeding out the bad stuff, thinning out the multitudes—"

"Spreading on the manure?" she asked sweetly, and then let out a stunned gasp as Hortense caught her from low and behind, sending her flying forward with a jolt into Matt. He caught hold of her firmly.

"Are you hurt?" he asked, concerned.

"Just my dignity," she said tightly, glaring back at Hortense, who was trotting to the far reaches of his chain lead with smug satisfaction.

"Who wants dignity? Your goat's got sense!" Matt laughed, grasping her long, thick braid and pulling her head back so he could kiss her soundly. Her ears rang. She gasped as he released her mouth only to kiss her again, the sensual onslaught parting her lips and sending her heart into a racing gallop.

He let go. "Uh-oh," he muttered grimly, his brows drawn together. He stepped away from her, his arms spread out gingerly as he opened his jacket and looked down at himself. He grimaced. Holding his coat flap, he tucked one hand into a pocket and drew out half an eggshell, dripping. A noticeable darkness was spreading.

"You were saying something about dignity and sense?" Annie said, laughing uncontrollably.

"So much for eggs Benedict." Matt sighed ruefully and turned his pockets inside-out to drain the oozing mess.

Annie knew she wasn't just attracted to Matt

Hagen. She really *liked* him. Any other man would have taken a stick to her goat.

Regaining her composure, she said, "Come on back to the house, and I'll clean your coat for you."

"What about me?" he said wickedly.

"I'll leave that chore to you."

10

ON MONDAY MORNING Matt left before dawn. When Annie heard an engine start, she thought she was dreaming, but when she got up in the morning, anticipating seeing Matt across the breakfast table, she found his door open, the room unoccupied, and an empty driveway. Depression set in.

So much for that, she thought. She should have known.

She got Katie off to school and went to work on her crafts, boxing for delivery what was finished and spending the rest of the morning painting watercolors of the barn.

The telephone rang just after noon.

"I'm not letting eight days pass without talking to you," Matt said, and her heart beat happily.

"I'm sorry I didn't see you off this morning," she replied, keeping her tone level.

"I peeked in on you and almost didn't leave," he said huskily. "Hmm, Annie, I miss you already." It

143

was on the tip of her tongue to ask him why he'd left so early if he felt that way. "Would you believe I'm working?" he asked with a low chuckle.

"Do you read minds?"

"No, but I'd like to get inside your head, among other places, and try to figure you out," he said seriously.

"I thought you already had."

He laughed softly, the sound stroking her senses into life. She closed her eyes and clutched the telephone. "Annie, Annie," he said seductively, "don't get so defensive with me. Listen, I had to leave before four in order to get back to the city in time for a meeting this morning."

"A meeting?" she said, almost believing. "Good for you." Then she frowned. "It's not safe to drive coast roads before dawn, Matt. There's fog as thick as pea soup some mornings."

"You're worrying about me. That's a good sign."

"I'd worry about any boarder," she said, and felt the silence at the other end of the line. "All right," she conceded. "I was worried."

"Hold the room for me this weekend."

Her heart drummed. "There's a couple coming up from San Jose. They reserved the room last May."

"Then the following weekend."

"Another reservation."

"Annie, I can't wait for three weeks to see you," he said in frustration.

"You've got your business, and I've got mine," she told him softly.

"Okay. I'll think of something."

She didn't hear from him the next day or the next.

She cut, sanded, painted, and packed up another reorder of elephant puzzles. She planned to take Katie out of school on Thursday to make the run down to Santa Rosa to drop off the order at the Coddingtown toy outlet.

She was out in the garden late Wednesday afternoon when she thought she heard the telephone ring. When she paused to listen, it was silent. She waited a moment for Katie to come outside to call her, but she didn't. Stifling disappointment, Annie went back to her weeding.

When she came inside, she asked Katie if there had been a telephone call. Katie looked up at her, wide-eyed. "No, I don't think so . . ." She went back to concentrating on her homework of printing her spelling words five times each.

They left at eight the next morning, winding down narrow Highway One to Stewarts Point, then cutting east to Geyserville. From there it was easy sailing by Highway 101 through the wine country to Santa Rosa.

Annie made her delivery by eleven in the morning, which gave her and Katie plenty of time to decide on a place for lunch.

"How about Chinese food, Katie?"

"No, let's go to Bob's Big Boy."

"But we go there every time. I can put this check in the bank, and we'll have a little extra to go someplace special today. Would you like some seafood?"

"No, I want to go to Bob's Big Boy."

"I thought Bob's Big Boy was *boring*," she said, mimicking Katie's tone teasingly.

"I changed my mind. Besides, I can get prawns there, Mommy." She looked down, her elfin face puckered with worry. "And we haven't got a lot of money, you know."

"Don't *you* start worrying about money," Annie said, wondering if her own concerns were rubbing off on her precious seven-year-old. "We have enough money to have Chinese food or seafood. Or how about pizza?"

Katie remained adamant. "Bob's Big Boy."

Annie sighed. "Oh, all right. Bob's it is, then."

They arrived just before the noon rush and were seated quickly in a comfortable booth in the non-smoking section at the back. They had hardly sat down before someone came up. Annie was concentrating on the menu. "We aren't ready to order yet, thank you," she said. She looked up—and gasped at the sight of Matt standing there, grinning roguishly down at her. He was wearing neat brown slacks and a lightweight yellow and brown shirt open at the collar. She could feel the warm flush flowing over her skin and the quick beat of her pulse.

"Fancy meeting you here," he drawled, his eyes dancing as he slid into the booth beside her, so close that his hip brushed firmly against hers. She inched back. Matt winked at Katie. "Good going, Kitten."

146

Katie grinned broadly.

Annie looked from one to the other as comprehension dawned. "I thought you were *working,*" she said stiffly.

"I took the afternoon off," he said casually, putting his hand on the vinyl seat back behind her shoulders. His fingers brushed her, sending a heated rush over her skin.

"Can I still have prawns?" Katie asked, looking at her mother's rigid face.

Annie forced a smile. "You can have anything you want, honey," she assured her, then cast Matt an accusing glare. His brows rose in question.

"What's the matter, Annie?"

"I'll talk to you about it later," she whispered tightly.

"Tell me now, or you'll spoil your appetite," he whispered, his eyes intent.

Katie looked at them both and went back to popping out the mask in the children's menu. She was worrying her lower lip nervously.

Matt shifted closer to Annie in order to reach into his slacks for some change. He held out some quarters to Katie. "Here you go, Katie. Play a couple of video games."

Her eyes brightened as she took the coins and scooted quickly out of the booth. "Getting rid of her?" Annie said, furious.

"No. I just don't want to put her in the middle of an argument, and you look ready to blow off some steam. Now, go ahead."

"You're the one who put my daughter in the middle," she said, anger boiling to the surface. "I don't like you involving Katie in your machinations. You put her in a position of having to lie to me to help you."

"Not a lie, a surprise. A pleasant one, I hoped."

"You *used* her."

Matt's eyes ignited, and his jaw went hard. "The way you are right now?" he ground out. "Putting her up as a wall between us? Every time I get close to you, you shove Katie out in front as a shield."

Annie bit down on her lower lip, knowing he was right. She looked across at her daughter, who was excitedly working the handle of a Pac-Man game, and felt her heart constrict. "It's not just that," she murmured huskily.

Matt let out his breath slowly, his anger dissipating. "I know, Annie. But I'm not your father. And I'm not your ex-husband. I have sins enough of my own without taking on theirs as well."

She looked up at him in surprised dismay, catching the ring of steel beneath his gentle tones.

"A mother should protect her child," he told her softly. "But ease up a little, Annie, or someday you'll lose her. She knows how I feel about you; I've made no secret of it. She's just trying to help nature along a little faster." His smile was tender. "Haven't you ever heard the old adage about the wisdom of dogs and children?"

She smiled faintly.

He searched her eyes. "I—" He glanced up sharply. The waitress was standing next to the booth. "We're not ready yet, thanks," he said politely, dismissing her. When she left, he gave Annie a rueful grin. "Hardly the place for world-shaking declarations," he whispered, his gaze holding hers. "Just trust me, Annie. I have your best interests at heart."

"And yours?"

"Especially mine," he agreed easily, his eyes glowing. "You didn't give me a chance to say it before you jumped on my case," he added, his eyes moving over her again, "but you look beautiful."

She was wearing a silk dress from her Sausalito days. It was sea-green, with a deeper-hued, tailored jacket that matched—one of the expensive brand-name fashions that Brent had bought for her. Even after seven years of infrequent wear, it hadn't gone out of style.

"And professional," he added in a whisper near her ear, sending chills along the curve of her neck. She remembered how it felt to have him kiss her there. She felt his hand barely touch her hair, which she had fixed in a heavy chignon instead of her usual waist-length braid. His light touch made her go all soft and warm inside, like freshly pulled taffy.

Katie slid back into the booth. "Can I have some more quarters, Matt? I used up all those."

He shook his head. "Six is enough, Kitten. Those games are addictive."

"Are you still mad, Mommy?"

"No. Good old Uncle Matt talked me out of it," she said, giving him a decidedly wicked look. Katie laughed.

"Witch," he said close to her ear. The waitress returned, and Katie ordered prawns. Annie opted for a chef's salad, while Matt decided on a hamburger.

"Since you took Katie out of school today, I think we should do something . . . educational," he remarked, his eyes twinkling across at Katie as she grimaced. "How about going to the Luther Burbank Gardens, then heading out to the Marianno Vallejo adobe?"

"Aw, gee," Katie groaned. "Do we have to? Mom's taken me to those places a *million* times."

"How about out to Glen Ellen to see Jack London's Wolf House?"

She shook her head decidedly.

"Armstrong Woods?"

"No."

Matt leaned forward, his forearms resting on either side of his plate, and growled in mock threat, "All right, you little wretch, what then?"

Katie giggled. She looked at Annie, and they both said, "A movie!"

Matt rolled his eyes. "Is that all? I thought you were going to say the aquarium."

Annie drew in a sharp breath and jabbed him hard in the ribs. He let out an equally sharp breath and added quickly, "But a movie it is." He grinned.

His van was parked beside Annie's Pinto. "What do

I do about my car?" she asked as he slid the van door back with a clang, and, with a grand gesture, invited Katie to jump into the back.

"Leave it," he told her. "I doubt anybody would want to steal it." He slid the door shut again and caught hold of Annie's hips. He bent to give her a quick, firm kiss on the mouth. "You in front with me, honey," he said devilishly.

As he started up the engine, he looked at her with dancing eyes. "Someday when Katie's playing at Suzanne's, I'll give you a real ride in the back," he said, giving her a seductive once-over before winking provocatively. He laughed softly. Annie's heart didn't stop racing for many, many blocks.

They decided on a Disney movie, *The Lady and the Tramp*. Matt bought a big bucket of buttered popcorn, sodas, chocolate Flicks, and two boxes of Ju-Ju-Beads. Katie was in seventh heaven.

"You're spoiling her," Annie whispered after they all sat down in the darkened theater, Matt in the middle.

He leaned close. "That's what little girls are made for, isn't it?" He caught her earlobe lightly between his teeth, making Annie almost jump out of her seat.

"Now look—" Annie reprimanded, her pulse racing.

"Why do you think I wanted to sit all the way in the back?" He grinned unrepentantly, his white teeth gleaming in the dim light. "Katie can watch the movie, and you and I can neck." He put his arm slowly around her shoulders, his eyes glinting with laughter.

"Will you behave?" she said, lifting his arm from her shoulders and putting his hand back in his own lap. "This is a public place."

"Public?" He made a sweeping glance around the near-empty theater. "Looks private enough to me." There were only six other patrons in the place and all of them were sitting near the front. He put his hand on her knee.

Heat traveled up her legs. She quickly picked up his hand and put it on his own knee. "Knock it off, Mr. Hagen, or I'll report you to the management," she said, laughing softly.

"Shhh," Katie hissed impatiently at both of them. "The movie's starting."

Annie and Matt looked at each other and laughed silently together.

Ten minutes into the movie, Matt put his arm around her again and offered her some popcorn. She took a handful. He wasn't the least bit interested in the movie, nor was she. But Katie was mesmerized by the big screen. If an earthquake hit, so long as the movie kept rolling, she wouldn't care about anything else.

Annie tried to concentrate on the story, but she already knew it, having seen it as a child herself. Lady and the Tramp were outside a restaurant eating spaghetti. They both got the same strand of pasta and ended up nose to nose. She dared a glance at Matt. He leaned toward her, and she slowly lifted her mouth. He kissed her, softly at first, then with growing desire, deepening the kiss gradually until the possession was full and her heart was thundering. She drew back slightly, breathless.

"Oh, Annie," he whispered against her temple, and she could hear the heightened pace of his breathing.

When he tried to kiss her again, she put her hand on his hard thigh and shook her head. His eyes softened in understanding, and he nodded. He moved his head closer to her ear and whispered, "Do you know any CPR?"

"No. Why?" she asked, confused.

"Because I may need it if you leave your hand where it is."

She snatched it away, and he laughed softly, leaning back in his seat to look at the movie screen.

It was still light outside when the movie finished. "Now where?" Matt said.

Annie glanced at Katie and caught her in the middle of a wide yawn. "Home, I think," she said. "It'll take at least two hours to get back, and by then it'll be dark." She didn't mention the fact that her car wasn't the most dependable, and that she didn't want to be stuck somewhere on a country road after nightfall.

Matt nodded. "Okay. I'll call you in a few hours to make sure you get home all right."

They did get home all right, and he did call. "I'll see you again on Saturday, Annie," he told her.

"We have guests coming, Matt. Remember?" she reminded him, wishing it were otherwise.

"I do, as it happens," he said grimly and then added on a lighter note, "I've still got my van."

But he called on Friday night to say he couldn't make it to Makawsa after all.

11

MATT CALLED YET again on Sunday night. "How was your weekend?"

His voice was enough to bring her whole body to life. "Fine."

"The couple from San Jose?"

"Spent most of their time fishing the Gualala. They didn't have much luck, unfortunately, but I think they enjoyed themselves. They've reserved the room for next September." Why was she jabbering?

"How's Katie?"

"She's right here, hanging on my arm, wanting to talk to you." She handed the receiver over to give herself a moment to calm down. She put her hand against her heart, trying to still its thundering beat. Katie spend several minutes on the telephone, then handed it back to Annie.

"He says he has a present for me," she said excitedly.

"I thought we talked about that," she told him quietly.

"Annie, I'm going to be traveling again for a while,"

he told her softly without arguing the previous issue.

Her heart sank. Wanderlust had struck him again. What could she say to that—enjoy yourself, Matt, when are you coming back to Makawsa, why do you have to go at all? So she said nothing.

"Annie?"

"Yes?"

A heavy silence lingered. "Say you miss me, Annie." His tone was deep, almost rough with constrained emotion.

"I do miss you, Matt." Too much of her feelings came through in those few words, and she closed her eyes.

"I won't be gone long."

He said nothing about where he was going or when he would be returning, and she didn't ask.

Ben and Bettie Metcalf arrived Friday afternoon. They were a retired couple who had both worked for more than thirty years for the postal system. They always stopped for a weekend at Makawsa on their way up the coast to see their children in Coos Bay, Oregon. They "dragged their feet" all the way from Los Angeles so they could "clean their lungs out." Since their first visit, three years before, it had been an annual stopover. Annie enjoyed their loquacious friendliness and always looked forward to their return visit in late October.

Saturday afternoon, while the Metcalfs were out walking in the woods, a silver-gray sports car pulled up Annie's driveway. She didn't recognize the make, but she'd never been that interested in fancy, expensive foreign sports cars. Brent had longed to own one, and probably did by now.

A tall man dressed immaculately in a pale blue shirt and tailored dark slacks and a vest rose from the vehicle. He straightened his tie and shrugged on a suit jacket as he walked toward the front steps. He had dark hair cut so perfectly that it looked like a cap on his head. His dark eyes were cold. His sweeping glance over her farmhouse and property made Annie stiffen.

"Is this Makawsa?" he asked as though he couldn't quite believe it.

"Yes. How can I help you?"

His hard gaze raked her from head to foot. She didn't like the way his eyes grew curiously speculative as he took in her braided hair, handmade bulky-knit cream sweater, jeans, and knee-high fringed moccasins.

"I'd like to speak with Matt Hagen."

"Mr. Hagen isn't here."

The man's brown eyes revealed his impatience. "Mrs. Seaton, I happen to know he comes up here to visit you. Now, this is important. I have to talk to him."

She stiffened at the implication. "Mr. Hagen isn't here," she repeated firmly, taking an immediate and immense dislike to the man.

"Where is he?"

"I have no idea."

He swore under his breath and looked around the place again, as though not believing her and expecting to see Matt somewhere nearby. His eyes pierced hers again. "When do you expect him?"

"I don't."

His mouth tightened, and a muscle worked slowly in his jaw. "All right, we'll play it your way," he said tautly, and reached into his inside jacket pocket to extract a business card. "If he calls, tell him I was here to see him." He came up the steps and handed her the card. She took it, but didn't bother to look at it. He stared into her cool eyes, and his brows flickered slightly. "If he comes, give it to him." She just looked at him. "Please," he added. "It's important, Mrs. Seaton."

"If he calls, I'll give him your message."

He went back down the steps. Glancing up at her again, he got into his sports car and drove off.

Just before dinner the same day, the telephone rang. Annie's heart leaped in hopeful expectation, but it was just the man who had called some days before—when Matt had been there—and asked where Makawsa was.

"Mrs. Seaton, I need to speak to Matt," he said without preamble.

How did he know her name? What was going on? "Mr. Hagen isn't here."

"Damn. Do you have any idea where he is? I've got to reach him."

"I have no idea. He doesn't answer to me," she said stiffly.

He sighed heavily. "Why does he do this to me?" he muttered in an undertone she was probably not meant to hear. "Mrs. Seaton, if he calls you, would you tell him I called?"

"I might if I knew who you were," she said pointedly.

He laughed. "Oh, sorry. I feel like we know each other. Jerry."

She jotted the name down on her pad. "Your number?"

"He's got it."

The Metcalfs departed in mid-afternoon on Sunday. Jerry whoever-he-was called again and asked if she had had any word from Matt. She said no.

Matt's blue van pulled up the driveway at just past six. Katie screeched with joy and raced down the steps, bouncing up and down in excitement outside the van door as Matt shut off the engine. He got out, laughing, and lifted her high into the air.

"What'd you bring me?" she cried.

"Oh, I forgot to bring it."

"You did not!" She grinned.

"Well, you can't do anything with it tonight, Kitten. It's almost dark," he reasoned, walking around to the other side of the van. He glanced up at Annie, and the impact of that intent, warm look made her remember the way he had said hello to her the last time. Her stomach curled tightly, and her mouth went dry.

Matt lifted out a sturdy, red-and-silver two-wheel bicycle.

"Oh, it's *beautiful!*" Katie cried joyously. "Oh, Mommy, it's just what I've always wanted. Oh, Matt, thank you, thank you!" she exclaimed, jumping up to hug him around the neck.

It cost too much, Annie thought grimly. She had looked at two-wheel bicycles because it was at the top of Katie's dream-list. She recognized the brand name of this one emblazoned down the brace bar and knew it had cost Matt almost two hundred dollars.

"I think Matt should put it back into his van where it'll be safe," Annie suggested.

He looked up at her with a faint frown. Katie protested immediately. "Can't I put it in my room tonight? *Please?*"

"A bicycle doesn't belong in the house. Matt, please?"

"You mom's right, Katie," he said, tweaking Katie's pigtail and lifting the bike back into the van.

"Be sure to lock the door so no one can steal my bike," Katie instructed proprietarily. Annie sighed. "Matt can read to me tonight, Mommy," Katie said, racing up the steps.

Matt came up the steps more slowly, his eyes holding hers. He cupped his big hand around the nape of her neck. "Don't argue with me about it, Annie," he said quietly.

"You know we can't accept something like that," she told him tautly, near tears at his generosity and out of distress at the prospect of facing Katie and telling her the gift couldn't be accepted. "Why did you do this, Matt?"

"Because I love her, and she wants a bike more than anything, and you can't afford one."

"Thanks." She tried to shrug off his hand.

It tightened, drawing her closer. "Dammit, Annie," he murmured roughly, "don't be so hardheaded." He bent his head and kissed her firmly.

She pulled back, determined to conquer the rising desire to fling herself into his arms, forget her principles, and kiss him back. "It's not right," she said, sticking to the issue.

"Why not?" he whispered hoarsely, starting to dip his head toward her again. Her heart raced.

She flattened her hand against his chest and felt the heavy beat of his heart against her palm. "You have people looking for you, by the way," she said, changing the subject.

He drew back and searched her eyes. "Who?"

She frowned at his angry expression. "Some man in a silver sports car and another named Jerry."

"Silver sports car," he said through his teeth. "He came up here?"

"Saturday afternoon."

"I'm sorry," he said, and raked his hand through his hair, his jaw clenched. "He must be pretty determined if he traced me up here." She'd never seen his eyes sparkle like that. "What did Jerry want?"

"I didn't ask. He said it was important that he reach you. The other man left his calling card. It's by the telephone in the foyer."

"Did you tell them I was coming up here?"

160

"I didn't know you were," she said defensively. "You said you were traveling again. That could have meant just about anything."

He tugged her braid hard, then kissed her soundly. "We'll just let them stew in their juices and wonder where I've disappeared to this time."

"They said it was important . . ." she managed to say breathlessly.

"Nothing is as important as this," he said, pulling her into his arms again to kiss her. When he stopped, she had forgotten all about the bike and the two men looking for him. Her lips were full and warm, and her breasts rose and fell heavily. Her body felt weighted with desire.

Matt passed his hand down over her hip as he looked into her smoky eyes. "I hope you'll always look at me as you are now," he whispered. "Annie, I—"

"Why aren't you two coming in?" Katie demanded. "I've been waiting and waiting . . ."

"I wanted to kiss your mom hello." Matt grinned at her over Annie's shoulder.

"Well, have you yet?" Katie giggled.

"Only once."

"Well, do it again and then come in and read to me," Katie said, staying to watch as Matt looked down into Annie's flushed face with a roguish gleam in his eyes.

"See? We've got her blessing," he said.

"Don't, Matt, please," she pleaded, but he did anyway. It was a quick, chaste kiss. Then he put his arm around her and guided her into the house.

As Matt read Katie a story, she kept interrupting to tell him one of the many things that had happened during his absence. Annie was amazed at his continued patience. When she tucked Katie in for the night, the little girl could talk of nothing but the new bike. She even mentioned it in her prayers. Annie didn't have the heart or nerve to tell her that she couldn't keep the gift.

She went back to the living room where Matt was sitting on the couch near the fire. He'd turned the lights down and put on a record. Soft music flowed to the staged background of thunder and a heavy downpour. It was one of her favorite albums, *Mystic Moods.*

Matt patted the seat beside him and smiled at her. She shook her head, not daring to get so close to him when he had that look in his eyes. He frowned.

"We have to talk about the bike, Matt," she said, sitting in the easy chair a safe distance from him.

"No, we don't. I'm not taking it back. That's final." He meant it.

She leaned forward. "Don't you see what's going to happen, Matt? If you bring her something every time you come up here, she'll begin to expect it. I don't want her to become that way. Other things in life are more important than bicycles and birds and lofts."

His expression softened. "You're right," he agreed. "I'm sorry." He put his head back and sighed heavily. "Part of the old life haunting me, I guess."

Her heart constricted with tenderness. He looked so

tired. Lines of tension were etched deep around his eyes. "Would you like some brandy?" she offered quietly.

"No, I want you," he said, looking at her.

She couldn't breathe for a moment. "If I sit next to you, I'm lost," she admitted huskily with a self-conscious smile.

"I won't do anything to you on this couch that Katie couldn't come in and watch," he told her seriously, understanding. "Just sit with me."

She came to him. He put his arm around her and pressed her firmly into his side. He sighed deeply, sounding immensely relieved.

"You can put your feet up on the coffee table if you want," she told him.

He did. After a moment he shifted downward so that his head could rest more comfortably against the back of the couch. He relaxed. In a few moments more she was sure he was asleep.

She leaned against him, her arm across his chest, her head resting there as well. She loved the feel of him. He was big, solid, warm, male. She reminded herself that she still knew very little about him. It was dangerous to feel this much for a virtual stranger. She drew back slowly and eased his arm from around her shoulders.

"Why'd you move away, Annie?" he whispered, and she wondered if he had been sleeping at all.

"Matt, you should turn in. You're beat."

"Maybe you're right," he agreed, his eyes sleep-dazed. He looked at her solemnly. "Annie, I'd give everything I own just to wake up to you every morning for the rest of my life."

"Grand sentiments. Come on, Mr. Hagen, off to bed."

Annie had to be firm with Katie to keep her off the bicycle the next morning. "You have five minutes to get down to the bus stop."

"Do I have to? Couldn't you call and say I'm sick? Please?" she pleaded.

"Absolutely not. Now, come on. Here's your lunch box."

"Aw, gee . . ."

"I love you, honey," Annie said, kissing her.

"Is Matt staying?"

"I don't know. I doubt he can, but he's not up yet to ask. Come on, I'll walk down with you." She ushered Katie out the front door before her daughter could think of another way to stall the inevitable.

She waved to Katie after she was sitting in the back of the little yellow school bus, then walked slowly back up the long drive, thinking about Matt. It would be the first time she'd been really alone with him. The thought filled her with tremulous excitement, liquid warmth, and overwhelming trepidation.

He was standing on the front porch holding a mug of steaming coffee. "Katie off to school?"

Her heart thumped nervously as she came up the steps. "Uh-huh. What would you like for breakfast?"

He gave her an amused look. "Alone at last, and you're scared to death."

"Waffles, since you can't fix those in your van." She went into the house.

Matt followed. "Make it scrambled eggs. That's simpler."

"You can have whatever you want," she said as she entered the kitchen.

"Can I?" he teased.

She blushed. "Almost," she corrected, going to the counter.

He laughed softly. Leaning against the counter, he watched her break fresh eggs into a bowl, pour in some cream, and whip them with a wire whisk. When butter had melted in the pan, she poured in the eggs and added grated cheese. She glanced up at him, wondering at his silence. He was frowning slightly, distant.

His eyes cleared as he realized she was looking at him.

He smiled. "Business," he said cryptically, and shrugged.

"What kind of business?" She had to know sometime.

"I'm selling a few things I don't need anymore."

"To the man in the silver sports car?"

His eyes glittered. "No."

"But he wants whatever it is you're selling, right?"

"Doesn't mean he'll get it," he said, and sipped his coffee. She scooped eggs onto a plate. "What about you?"

"I ate with Katie."

165

"Sit with me, Annie."

She did, clasping her hands together on the table and watching him curiously. "What do you do for a living, Matt?"

He frowned slightly and glanced up at her. He finished a bite of eggs before answering. "I guess you could say I'm in real estate." He lifted his mug and studied her over the rim before sipping.

She sensed his reticence and immediately pulled back. He didn't want to tell her. She held back more questions, feeling hurt.

"I'm not cutting you off," he told her, reaching out to put his hand over hers. "Its just that . . . it's a little complicated. I don't know how much you're ready to—"

She withdrew her hands and stood to clear his dishes. "I understand."

"No, you don't," he said harshly, standing up. She moved away from him. He came up behind her at the sink. "Annie . . ."

"You don't have to tell me anything," she told him too quickly, suddenly not wanting to know. She couldn't even decipher her reasons.

He put his hands on her hips. She tensed. "Just leave everything," he murmured roughly. "Let's go out for a walk."

Her breath was shallow, her body warm and full of longing. She swallowed hard. "I . . . I should do the dishes."

"Forget the dishes," he whispered raggedly and drew her back against him. One hand came around in front of her and traveled upward to cup a full breast. She drew in a sharp breath and leaned back, her head resting against the curve of his neck.

"Annie, if we stay inside, I'm going to make love to you. Are you ready for that?" he asked, the soft timbre of his voice sending waves of desire through her.

"I . . . I don't know, Matt," she admitted truthfully.

"Then we've got to go for a walk." He let her go reluctantly.

They walked along the river, Matt stooping every so often to pick up rocks to skip across the water. He said very little, filled with thought. He seemed grim. She didn't ask questions.

He paused once and looked at her solemnly. "I meant what I said last night."

She didn't pretend not to remember. He'd said he'd give anything to wake up with her for the rest of his life. It had been all she could think about last night as she lay alone in her bed, Matt just down the hall from her. "It's too early to talk about it."

As they wandered along the wooded trail, she picked flowers. After a long while, she found they had walked all the way around and up the long trail to the meadow above Makawsa, where she and Katie went for their private Sunday worship and where Matt had shared his fantasy.

"Instinct," he said softly.

"Matt . . ." It was her fault they had come this way, she knew. He was right, however: instinct. She wanted him so badly she had stopped thinking of consequences. Was it all a mistake after all?

"I love you, Annie," he said, coming close. She was almost paralyzed with shyness. He cupped her face gently in his hands. "I love you," he repeated, and kissed her very gently.

The flowers in her hand fluttered to the ground as she sank heavily against him, embracing him, tilting back her head and returning his kiss with all the passion she had held in check during the last weeks.

His hands ran down her back and over her buttocks, arching her forward as he moved his hips in a slow rhythmic motion against hers. She moaned softly, her head going back, and he kissed the warm, sensitive skin of her throat.

"I know it's too soon for you," he rasped softly, "but I can't wait, Annie. You've got to trust that I won't hurt you."

She could scarcely breath, her heart was racing so fast.

"Oh, Annie, you feel so good . . ."

Her tunic fell away, then her thin bra, his Pendleton shirt, his T-shirt.

The crisp male hair on his chest felt like a thousand caresses against her breasts and taut nipples. Her knees felt weak; her legs trembled. Desire that had long been dammed up inside her was pouring over all her inner barriers. Matt laid her down on the soft grass and took off her moccasins, then eased down her jeans and cotton panties.

She heard the hiss of his zipper and the rush of

denim. Turning her head slowly, she dared to open her eyes and look up at him. Her mouth felt parched at the sight of his unhidden virility and the burning, fierce look in his eyes as he bent down to her.

He raised himself onto his elbow and looked into her eyes. "What is it?" he asked softly.

She shook her head, speechless.

He raised himself a little more and leaned across to kiss her in a gentle unhurried way. "Trust me, Annie," he murmured against her lips. She felt his strong hand make a slow caress from her collarbones to her quivering thighs. She closed her eyes tightly and held her breath.

"I'm so scared," she admitted shakily.

"I know," he whispered.

"I—I don't know why . . ."

"Yes, you do, Annie. It's been a long time, and you're surrendering yourself again."

She searched his blue eyes, some of her fear leaving her at what she saw glowing there. He lowered his head slowly and ran his tongue around one nipple. Her back arched, and she closed her eyes, her lips parting.

His hand was warm on her thigh. "Relax," he murmured, kissing her breast again, open-mouthed, rubbing very gently with the edge of his teeth. He kept stroking her thigh, tenderly, slowly, until her muscles eased. Then his hand moved upward. She drew in her breath. "It's all right," he whispered. Fiery heat shot through her body at his voluptuous massage. It was happening so fast.

"Oh, Matt . . ."

"You don't have to fight it."

She made a soft whimpering sound in the back of her throat. He parted her lips fiercely and kissed her. She put her arms around his shoulders and pressed him to her almost frantically.

"Oh, Annie, it's going to be perfect . . ."

She felt the hard, hot flesh of his thighs between hers and his hands making a firm caress down her body. He raised her hips slightly and gripped her thighs. She raised her knees and heard his hoarse exclamation. He lifted himself above her, his arms bracing his weight off her.

They looked into each other's eyes as he eased carefully inside her. Watching the muscles in his face tighten with restrained passion, she ran her hand along the firm flesh of his chest and ribs. He closed his eyes and gritted his teeth, his chin lowering as he fought for control.

"I love you," she whispered, knowing her power over him. His own was just as great.

He began the deep stroking inside her body, slowly at first, carefully, until she adjusted to him and began her own answering rhythm. Her body quivered as sensation peaked. Her head thrashed from side to side. She clutched wildly at him, as if to still the excruciating pain-pleasure of his possession, and felt instead the hard male muscles tense and relax, tense and relax in quickening demand. A shuddering moan began deep inside her, and his own moan followed, sending doves into startled flight from a nearby tree.

Matt gasped for air, his body shaking violently. Slowly he relaxed against her, then started to roll her over to take his considerable weight from her.

"No," she protested thickly, holding him tightly. "I want to feel your weight on me and you inside me awhile longer."

He propped himself up on his elbows and gently caressed the damp tendrils of hair back from her flushed cheeks. He kissed her slowly. "I can't leave you anyway," he whispered hoarsely, smiling slightly, and she felt the slow, profoundly awakening movement of his hips against hers as his eyes narrowed again in glazed passion. It began again slowly, but the crescendo was no less earth-shattering.

Annie felt drowsy in the mid-morning sunlight that filled the meadow. She watched Matt pick up one flower at a time and array her slender, pale body like an altar of worship. He touched her everywhere and kissed her often. He ran a flower across her brow. "You said you loved me."

She smiled, saying nothing.

He bent over her and kissed her long and tenderly. She ran her hands lovingly down his smooth, hard back. He nuzzled her neck. "Annie, were you safe?"

She frowned. It was a moment before she understood, and her breath stopped. He raised up to look down at her. "Don't look so worried. It's all right."

"I . . . I didn't even think of it."

"Maybe I should have, but I didn't."

She searched his eyes, warm and still faintly hazy with spent passion.

How could she have been so foolish as not to have considered the possibility of getting pregnant? She had spent one entire marriage being careful, taking responsibility for birth control, worrying about it, finally getting caught anyway, and having her rose-colored glasses shattered.

"Annie, don't look like that. I can't think of anything I'd like better than making a child with you," he told her seriously.

Her eyes filled with tears. "Certain things should happen first."

"Are you angling for a proposal?" he teased.

She shook her head, aching inside with doubt.

Matt searched her eyes, the teasing glint replaced by a dark, half-desperate look. "Annie, I've wanted to marry you since the first moment I saw you standing barefoot in your garden. Everything I'm doing now is paving my way to that."

12

THE TELEPHONE WAS ringing when they came up the front steps several hours later. Annie quickened her pace. "Don't answer it, Annie. Just let it ring."

She glanced back at his glowering expression. "I

have to. It could concern Katie." Or a possible guest, or any one of the shops with which she did business.

He nodded grimly.

It was Jerry again, and her heart felt like a heavy stone in her chest. Not knowing what to say, she looked miserably at Matt and mouthed "Jerry" as he came in the door. His expression was grim as he walked across to her holding out his hand.

"What is it, Jerry?" he said flatly, turning his back to her.

She should have let it ring. She went into the kitchen to do the breakfast dishes and saw by the sunflower wall clock that it was almost two o'clock. Katie would be home in little more than an hour.

Matt came in. "I've got to leave."

She nodded, expecting it. Her eyes burned. Questions kept popping into her head. Who *was* Jerry? Who was the man in the silver sports car? Why did Matt have to leave now, after such a miraculous morning in the meadow, when her body was still warm and richly sated? What was he really selling?

Remembering his manner that morning, and his remark that everything was "complicated," she was afraid he wouldn't tell her. Then what? Tell me what's going on and what you're doing, or never come back! Could she say that, feeling as she did about him?

He stood behind her and put his hands on her shoulders, and she felt her throat closing up. *Separation.* She was beginning to wait for his returns. But were they ever really together, except in that wonderful physical way they had been today? What did she really know about Matt Hagen? He drove a blue van, his time was his own, he was in real estate, and two men were looking for him, one of whom she distrusted on sight, the other she knew nothing about. It wasn't much on which to build trust.

Yet she was in love with him.

"Annie . . ." He turned her around to face him. "It won't always be this way."

"What way?"

"Me coming and going like a free agent. I'm not. I'm caught between two worlds right now. I've got to clear myself of one before I can live fully in the other."

"I don't really know much about you, do I?" she said with difficulty, searching his eyes.

He frowned slightly, saying nothing for a long moment. He kissed her and held her close. "You know everything about me that counts for anything. Just remember that."

He didn't take the bike with him when he left.

Annie didn't hear from Matt for three days. Then he called late, long after Katie was in bed and Annie herself had been working on some plaques. "I just wanted to hear your voice," he said, sounding tired and low.

"Where are you, Matt?" she asked, so lonely for him that her soul ached.

"In the city. I'd give you a number, but I'm not going to be here much longer." He sighed heavily. "Annie . . ." If he'd been in the same room, they would be making love, she knew. It was amazing how one half-whispered word could say so much.

"Nothing's easy, is it?" he said vaguely, almost to himself. The silence lengthened. He seemed to be waiting for her to speak.

"Matt, I love you."

"That's what I needed to hear," he said softly.

She had to grit her teeth to keep from asking him if he would be up for the weekend, and he said nothing about it.

Harry and Agnes Oleson of New York arrived. Annie suspected they were going to be difficult when Harry Oleson opened the trunk of his Seville and left it to her to carry in their four suitcases. Within the first hour of their stay, Annie knew it was going to be a very long weekend. She kept Katie out of the way as much as possible, since both of the Olesons seemed to abhor the presence of children. Annie was glad she had raised the room rent to sixty-five dollars a night, knowing she was going to have to work extra hard.

"There's no television set in our room," Harry complained. "I'd like to know what's going on in the world."

"Oh Harry, why do you want to hear the news? We're supposed to be on vacation," his wife said in a grating whine.

"You're just too stupid to care what's going on," her husband retorted. "You haven't looked at a newspaper since Orphan Annie retired. All you're ever interested in is bridge and the latest sale at Saks."

The heavyset woman, with pale blue eyes in a face that must have once been quite beautiful, sat forward on Annie's couch. "Don't you call me stupid. Just because I don't rub my hands together over the latest terrorist activity in the Middle East doesn't mean I don't know what's going on!"

"Oh, shut up, Agnes," he said wearily. "Do you have a radio?" he demanded of Annie.

"Yes. Right over there," she answered calmly.

"Turn it on for some news," he ordered. "And get me a drink. Bourbon on the rocks."

"Drink wine, Harry," Agnes said nastily. "You always get mean when you drink bourbon."

They traded spiteful words constantly over the dinner table while Annie and Katie ate cautiously in the kitchen. The roast was too well done for Harry and too rare for Agnes. The coffee wasn't strong enough and it was the wrong brand, and why didn't Annie have mocha mix instead of cream, which was so fattening. Agnes argued that it was Harry's idea to stay in the woods, and Harry blamed his lack of a television set on Agnes.

Annie's head was splitting by the time she tucked Katie in at eight o'clock and explained regretfully that she couldn't read this evening. She couldn't linger either because Harry Oleson rapped loudly at the door and ordered crème de menthe for Agnes.

On Annie's way into the living room, the telephone rang. It was Matt. Relief and joy surged inside her at the sound of his voice.

"How's your weekend?" he asked softly, a seductive question in his tone.

"Fine," she lied, thinking of the hellish afternoon and evening she had spent catering to unreasonably difficult guests. She glanced worriedly toward the couple, who were arguing loudly in her living room.

"What's going on?" Matt asked, undoubtedly hearing some of the ruckus.

"Nothing," she said, grateful that the Olesons had momentarily lapsed into tense, angry silence.

"I'm sorry I couldn't make it up this weekend. I've got an important meeting with a prospective buyer tomorrow morning."

Harry came and stood in the archway. "What about that crème de menthe?" he demanded rudely.

"I'll be with you in just a moment, Mr. Oleson," Annie said, cupping her hand over the receiver, trying to block his voice from Matt's hearing.

But Matt had already heard it. "What's going on, Annie?"

"I have guests, Matt. I'm sorry, I can't talk. Thank you for calling."

She served the Olesons their drinks, then found herself dragged into their argument about how far it was to Fort Bragg and how long it would take to get there. Agnes became smug when Annie's information confirmed her beliefs, and Harry claimed that she probably didn't know anything anyway. "There's nothing in Fort Bragg. We'll drive down to Santa Rosa and head back to San Francisco."

"You *promised* Harry!" Agnes wailed angrily. "We're going to ride that Skunk Train through the redwoods."

Annie wondered if she could survive them until Sunday morning when they'd be leaving. They were still arguing on the way down the hall to their bedroom.

Annie took a couple aspirin and went to bed after an hour of painting in her workroom. She set her alarm for five o'clock, sure the Olesons would be on the warpath again in the morning. She wanted to have a clear head by the time they got up and began their endless demands.

The next morning, she got up, showered, dressed, and braided her hair before going into the darkened kitchen to set up the coffee. She started a fire in the living room before sitting down to read her morning devotions.

Someone tapped lightly on the front door. Startled, she went to the window first to peep outside, and saw Matt's van parked beside the Olesons yellow and white Cadillac Seville.

"Matt," she whispered in surprise, opening the door quickly. "What are you doing here?"

He came in and closed the door quietly behind him before pulling her into his arms and kissing her hungrily. She was breathless when he stopped. Her face was lightly burned from his stubbled chin. "I got here about two in the morning," he whispered hoarsely against her hair. "You sounded upset last night. What's up?"

"Last night? You camped outside in your van? You said you had a meeting . . ."

He chuckled at her rambling words. Both of them knew why she was flustered. He cupped her breast. "I thought about coming in and sleeping with you," he murmured seductively, his thumb stroking her nipple. "But didn't"—he kissed her—"want to"—he kissed her again—"shock your guests," he whispered hoarsely. "Oh, Annie, I need you. Can you tell?" He kissed her urgently, tasting the sweetness of her mouth with its tang of toothpaste.

Her arms slid around him as she kissed him back, happy to see him again.

He dragged his mouth away after a long, throbbing moment and whispered raggedly, "Come out to my van and we'll welcome the sunrise in a pagan ritual."

She laughed softly at his teasing and shook her head. He rubbed his hips against hers. "What do I do about this?" he growled against her ear.

"I know what I wish you could do," she murmured, trying to keep her head. "What about your meeting?"

"I canceled it. If they're really interested, they'll wait a day or two." He regarded her seriously. "You're not going to tell me what was going on?"

"Nothing much." She grimaced expressively. "Would you like some coffee and breakfast?"

"Strudel." He winked, his eyes sparkling, his hand smoothing down her slender hip. When she twisted away from his questing hand, he laughed softly and caught hold of her again, pulling her back into his arms.

Unexpectedly the Olesons' bedroom door opened. Annie stiffened and pushed quickly back from Matt. He gave her a curious look and then leaned indolently against the living room arch to watch her in amusement.

Agnes was lumbering down the hall in curlers and a long red satin bathrobe. "Harry wants coffee and an Alka-Seltzer," she said to Annie without even coming to the end of the hallway. "I want a cheese omelette, three strips of bacon, and buttered toast. Oh, and orange juice, fresh orange juice." Heading back the way she had come, she grumbled, "You should have a bell in our room so I don't have to come looking for you."

Annie glanced at Matt in embarrassment and saw the hard, angry look in his eyes.

"And orange juice," Agnes called again before closing the door.

"Why did you let her talk to you like that?" Matt demanded, his eyes glittering dangerously as he glared down the hall.

"She's a guest." He started to say something, and she touched his arm. "We all do what we have to to make a decent living."

Matt sat at the kitchen table while Annie whipped eggs for an omelet. Harry Oleson was calling for her. She set the bowl down, wiped her hands on her apron, and passed Matt to go out into the hall.

"The hot water gave out."

"I'm sorry," Annie apologized, knowing there'd been more than enough for two fifteen-minute showers.

"Sorry isn't much good. Is breakfast ready yet? We want to drive down to Fort Ross."

"Harry!" Agnes called angrily.

He swore under his breath and marched back into the bedroom, slamming the door behind him.

Katie came out of her bedroom, rubbing her eyes and looking confused. "Mommy?"

"It's all right, honey. Come on into the kitchen." Annie hurried Katie along, not wanting her around the Olesons at all. When Katie saw Matt sitting in the kitchen, she smiled brightly and crawled up onto his lap to snuggle close. "Did you bring me something?" she asked.

Annie gave him a pointed look. He lightly tugged Katie's straggly pigtail. "Not this time, Kitten."

"I'm glad you're here," she murmured, still half asleep. Matt winked at Annie. Looking at them together, she felt a pang.

The Olesons arrived in the dining room just as Annie had everything ready for them. Agnes muttered complaints about the shower, the kind of soap Annie had laid out, and the owl that had kept her up all night with its endless hooting in a tree outside. Harry told her to shut up and eat if she wanted to see Fort Ross.

"This doesn't taste like fresh orange juice," Harry said with a grunt as Annie replenished his coffee cup.

"Make some more. This is too watery."

Matt came abruptly through the swinging door of the kitchen and planted his hands on the table between the two guests. He looked from Harry to Agnes coldly and said very softly, "When you finish your breakfast, pack your bags and take off."

"Matt—" Annie said weakly, appalled.

"No one treats you like this," he told her, brooking no argument.

"Now, just a damn minute," Harry Oleson blustered, tossing down his linen napkin like a flung gauntlet. "We paid to stay here. And who the hell are you?"

Matt reached into his back pocket, extracted his old wallet from his jeans, opened it, and took out four twenties. "For your inconvenience," he snarled, stuffing them into the empty orange-juice glass. "And one minute is just about all the time you've got, buster, before I throw you out that door."

Harry Oleson looked into Matt Hagen's blazing blue eyes and stood up. "Come on, Agnes. We're leaving." He extracted the money from the glass with shaky fingers, then pulled his wife's chair back hastily, and prodded her out of the room while trying to shush her rebellious tongue.

Annie put a trembling hand to her cold cheek. "You had no right to do that," she said faintly, horrified at the scene.

"I had the right of a man who loves you," he retorted, furious.

"I've never been so embarrassed," she said, shaking

violently. "Part of my living comes from having guests here on weekends. I can stand a little rudeness for a day or two."

"Well, if it's only money you're worried about, *I'll* pay for the room."

Her eyes welled with hurt tears. She hastily piled the dishes onto a tray and brushed past him into the kitchen. "Annie," he said with a groan. Katie was standing just inside the kitchen door, staring from Annie to Matt, her eyes wide with fright and worry. "Mommy? Matt?"

"It's okay, Kitten. Why don't you go get dressed, and we'll take a walk for a while and let your mom sort some things out."

Annie gave her daughter a wobbly smile and a nod, and carried the tray of dirty dishes to the sink. Katie left through the swinging door.

Matt came up behind Annie as she ran water in a loud rush into the sink. He put his hands on her waist. "Just go away, Matt," she choked out.

"I'm sorry. I didn't mean that. Annie, don't expect me to stand around while some jerk treats you like his personal slave. I can't, and I won't."

She closed her eyes tightly. He had left the city to drive all the way back to Makawsa just because he had sensed she was upset last night. He had canceled an important meeting to come and see if she was all right. Then, when he'd overheard her guest being rude to her, he'd evicted them and paid them back out of his own pocket. In defense of her. How could she be angry with him for caring so much?

"It's not just the money," she managed to say past the heavy, painful lump in her throat.

"I was angry when I said that." He moved closer, sliding his hands around her middle, drawing her gently back against him.

"This is still my house, Matt, and it was my decision to make, not yours."

She let out a shaky sigh when he said nothing to that. His hands massaged her waist, and after a moment she leaned back against him, knowing it was a moot issue. He belonged here now just as much as she did. But her emotions were in such a tangle.

Matt rested his chin lightly on her hair. "You're right, Annie. It was for you to say. Why don't I ask the Olesons to stay? Then you can have the honor of throwing them out."

She laughed, raising a shaky hand to wipe away tears.

Matt turned her around and tipped up her chin gently. He frowned when he saw her pale face and tear-soaked eyes. "It's a lot more than the Olesons or me stepping in. You're not sure of anything right now, are you?"

"I'm not even sure of myself," she admitted, letting her full vulnerability show.

"You can be sure of me, Annie. Keep telling yourself that."

After the Olesons departed, Matt took Katie out for a

walk, and Annie changed the linens and towels in the guest room. She vacuumed, dusted, washed the windows, and put fresh flowers in the room just to be sure the aura of the Olesons was completely gone.

Matt and Katie stayed outside for a long time. When Annie finally went out to look for them, she saw them coming up the driveway. She waved.

"Katie was showing me some special places," Matt told her with an indulgent smile. "I didn't know she was taking me so far afield. Were you worried?"

"A little," Annie admitted.

"Look what we caught," Katie said, opening her cupped palms to show her mother a small lizard. "Matt said I could keep it long enough to show you." She put it down and watched it scurry through the grass looking for a place to hide.

They all walked back to the house together. "You'd never leave this place, would you, Annie?" he said softly, putting an arm around her shoulders.

"No. I couldn't." She looked up at him. "I guess I'm just like that hermit crab Katie found at the beach."

Katie was running ahead of them with boundless energy. Annie sighed. "Sometimes Katie doesn't like it here, I know, but it's the best place in the world to grow up."

"I happen to agree with you," he said quietly, "but it just means we have to wait. And that's damn hard."

When they reached the front steps, the telephone was ringing. Matt's arm tightened briefly before he let her go.

It was Jerry again. Annie held out the telephone. Matt kissed her lightly on the mouth before taking it. When she started to walk away, he caught her hand and tugged her back. "What is it, Jerry?" He looked into Annie's eyes and mouthed, "I love you."

His eyes narrowed sharply as he listened. "I know, Jerry. Couldn't be helped." He let go of Annie reluctantly. "It's not something I want to do, no," he said, brows drawn. He listened again, his expression suddenly lightening. "That's different." He glanced quickly at his watch. "I can make it back by seven this evening."

Annie's heart sank to the soles of her feet. He was leaving again. How long could she continue this way, with him coming and going and her never knowing when she'd see him again?

He laughed. "Jerry, I'm as sure about this as I am that there's going to be a sunrise tomorrow. Make it Jack's restaurant at eight. See you there."

He turned to Annie and swept her up in a bold bear hug, kissing her hard. "This could be it! Oh, Lord, woman, I love you!" He kissed her again, parting her lips and delving hungrily into her mouth. "Wish me luck," he said thickly when he finally let her go.

"Always," she managed to say shakily.

"Katie!" he called. She came on the run. "Gotta hit the road, Kitten." He picked her up and hugged her. "Take care of your mom for me, all right? I'll be back in a few days."

But what did a few days mean?

Katie squeezed him around the neck and kissed him. "Okay."

Annie walked out to his van with him. He felt her unhappy silence. "Annie, this could be the biggest deal I've ever made. The coup de grace." He stroked her cheek. "Don't worry so much. If it goes through the way I want, I'll explain everything to you on my next visit. We'll start to make our own plans."

She nodded, unable to speak.

He frowned. Drawing her close, he covered her mouth in a heady kiss, his tongue plumbing the sweetness of her mouth while his hands caressed her from her shoulders to her hips and back up again. Then his hands cupped her face so he could look solemnly down at her, his eyes burning with passionate tenderness. "Maybe I've handled things wrong, I don't know. But you're not like anyone I've ever met before, Annie. And I've tried to go carefully with you so I wouldn't scare you off."

She searched his face, trying to understand what he was trying to tell her.

"Just keep the home fires burning for me," he told her and left.

13

THREE DAYS LATER, Marsha and Suzanne arrived for a surprise afternoon visit. As soon as the girls dashed off to play, Marsha reached into the back seat of her station wagon and hauled out a big pile of newspapers. She carried them into the house, Annie watching quizzically, and put them down on the coffee table, where Annie had set a tray with coffee and a plate of cookies.

"I just knew his name sounded familiar," Marsha said, spreading half a dozen newspapers across the polished tabletop.

"What is all this, Marsha?"

"Just look. Is this the same Matthew Hagen who's been coming up here, Annie?" she asked anxiously, tapping a picture on the front page of one of the newspapers.

Annie glanced down and saw Matt. He looked so different dressed in a three-piece business suit that she almost didn't recognize him. He was standing with two other men of the same bold breed. "Yes," she said, staring, a feeling of dread already sinking into the pit of her stomach. The Matt in the picture was hard-looking, his smile faintly sardonic, his expression shrewd.

"Lord, Ted will shoot him on sight if he comes back

up here," Marsha muttered, mentioning her easygoing forester husband. "Do you know what he does?" she asked, tapping Matt's picture.

"He said he was in real estate."

"Oh, is that all?" Marsha said. "Annie, he was involved in all sorts of deals in the Bay Area—office buildings, apartment complexes, you name it. This man here is one he got elected to some commission or other so he could have a few zoning laws conveniently changed to his benefit. And that man is probably another shady character. Just read the whole bunch, Annie," she said, and plunked down dismally into a chair.

"Where did you get all these newspapers?" Annie asked faintly, trying to think straight. From the dates, she saw that some of them were more than two years old. In fact, none was more recent than eighteen months ago. She was trying desperately to make sense of it all and get her wind back after the blow of Marsha's implications. What was all this, anyway? What did it mean?

"Ted saves everything to recycle," Marsha explained. "Cans, bottles, newspapers. He would recycle me if he could. He's had these papers stacked in our garage for a hundred years it seems! And a good thing, I guess. Annie, what's Hagen doing up here in Gualala?" she asked, worried. "He isn't planning to buy some coast property, then sell it off to some developer who'll build some hideous planned community, is he? He'd better not be!" she declared, incensed at the very idea.

"I . . . I don't really know," Annie admitted. "He just comes to see me and Katie."

"Baloney!" Marsha snapped. She gestured derisively at the papers. "That kind of wheeler-dealer doesn't even take a vacation, let alone idle time away. A man like him doesn't marry, he *merges.* He's got another reason for coming up here. Oh, Lord, why our beautiful Gualala?" She sat forward intently. "We should have laws like Oregon where the state owns all the coastal property and no one can build on it. That way it stays the way it is, and *everyone* enjoys it. But California? No such luck. Whoever has the bucks gets the land, and then they build some big monstrosity on it, and *no one* can see around it to the real beauty we have." She shook her head. "The whole idea of more housing makes me absolutely sick."

It made Annie sick, too. Surely Matt couldn't be planning such a thing!

By the time Marsha left with Suzanne, Annie's head was pounding with a tension headache, and she was close to tears. If she'd known where to reach Matt, she would have called him and asked him to explain it all to her first hand. Since she couldn't reach him, she knew she would have to read all the newspapers Marsha had dumped on her table and try to sort things out for herself. She stacked the papers and hid them in a closet until after Katie had had her bath and eaten her dinner and was tucked safely into bed.

After making herself comfortable in the living

room, Annie put all the newspapers in chronological order and began with one four years old. Marsha must have scrounged through all of her husband's piles to dig all these up, she thought, almost angry at the effort. She had even gone so far as to put paper clips on the pages that mentioned Matt and circle the stories in red ink, as well as adding her own bold remarks alongside.

The first article Annie read connected Matt with a seaside condominium development south of San Francisco. Citizens were up in arms because it would block the view of existing homes. Another newspaper had Matt on the society page beside his wife, Veronica, a socialite and the daughter of a prominent commissioner. Veronica Hagen was gorgeous in a chic, well-bred way that advertised both money and class. Her dark hair was fashionably cut and her elegant figure was perfectly displayed in a designer gown. Matt, devastating in a tuxedo, had an arm around her waist as they were coming out of the Geary Theatre after the opening of *A Chorus Line.*

Annie thought of herself in her faded granny dress, her hair in a behind-the-times plait down her back, and working barefoot in her flower garden. She looked at Veronica again—sleek, confident, smiling proudly up at Matt, as though he were a live trophy on her arm.

Annie studied Matt, looking so elegant in formal clothes, his head high. gazing impatiently into the camera lens. How could this be the same man who had driven up her driveway in that dented blue van, wearing dirty hiking boots, faded jeans, and an old fatigue jacket from army days?

Annie felt sick. Worse, she felt betrayed.

From the pile of newspapers she learned that Matt had had his finger in every pie. He'd been involved in land development in Silicon Valley, the social scene, and politics. That was apparently where his problems had started, for the last few articles mentioned an investigation into government kickbacks, naming a company Matt Hagen owned. The last newspaper mentioned his "disappearance."

She could sure pick men.

Annie thought back to all the things he had said about himself. *Clearing the dust . . . living on my laurels . . . in real estate . . .* She thought of the distasteful man in the silver-gray sports car and recognized him as the man in the first picture Marsha had showed her. She remembered Matt's words before he'd left: "It could be the biggest deal I've ever made!" And she realized she made the second biggest, most painful mistake of her life by falling in love with him!

The next morning she was bleary-eyed with exhaustion when Katie got up to get ready for school. "Mommy, what's wrong?"

"Just a cold, honey." It was all she could do to keep the tears at bay until Katie was on her way to the bus stop. What was she going to do about Katie?

She tried to work and botched the two watercolors of the barn. Her hand was shaking too much to control the delicate strokes of her tole painting. She looked at all the little boxes and bowls of seeds, pods, and cones and had to leave the room before she succumbed to the urge to sweep them all onto the floor in a fit of hurt hysteria.

Even a long walk along the Gualala failed to cheer her. She kept looking at the water and remembering Matt skipping stones with Katie. Everywhere she looked reminded her of Matt.

Oh, Lord, what could she say to Katie when Matt stopped coming?

She sat in the meadow above the farmhouse, her head in her hands, sobbing, trying to obliterate the memory of him making love to her. Maybe he did love her, but it didn't change what he was. Had he been traveling around just until things cooled down enough for him to return to the city?

Why did she fall in love with men who lacked character? Brent had been bad enough, but Matt . . .

She clenched her fists, her mouth working as tears coursed down her pale cheeks, and burning anger filled her. She remembered Brent as he'd been when she'd first met him, and the way he'd become later. Matt Hagen was a hundred times worse. Wheeler-dealer, Marsha had said. What an understatement! Annie's old disillusionment paled compared to this new blow to her self-confidence. How could she have been so blind?

She wouldn't cry for Matt Hagen! He wasn't worth it!

But when he called on Thursday night, she almost did.

She was in her workroom when the phone rang. She'd taken everything from the shelves and stacked it on the table and floor so she could dust and resort—hoping the time-consuming job would keep her mind off Matt. She suspected the call was from Marsha, asking if she had heard anything from Matt.

"Katie, if it's Marsha again, tell her I'll call back tomorrow," Annie called.

The phone stopped ringing, and she heard Katie's excited exclamation. Matt! Rubbing her hands free of furniture oil and biting down hard on her lower lip, she tried to still the thunderous beat of her heart.

"Mom's had an awful cold all week," Annie heard Katie saying. "Her nose is all red, and her eyes are all puffy. She—"

"Let me have the telephone, Katie. You go to your room for a few minutes."

"But I want to talk to Matt," Katie protested.

It would be the last time she ever spoke with him so Annie let her. When she took the receiver, she wondered vaguely what Matt had said to make Katie's face light up.

"Hello," she said brittlely, putting a calming hand on Katie's head and nodding toward her room down the hall.

"How would you like to be Mrs. Matt Hagen by the end of next week?" he asked, laughing softly.

Her knuckles whitened on the telephone receiver. "Not much," she said.

Silence. "What did you say?" he said blankly.

"Just a minute," she told him, cupping her hand over the receiver. "Katie, please go to your room. This is private."

"He said he's going to marry you, Mommy! That'll make him my daddy, won't it?"

"Katie, go to your room, please."

Katie frowned, searching her eyes. Confused, she did as she was asked. Annie waited until the bedroom door was shut. She was afraid her throat would close up entirely and choke her before she could say what she had to.

"Annie? What's going on?"

His gentle tone aroused her anger. "A neighbor brought over a stack of newspapers for me to read."

He sighed heavily, and she felt a hopelessness she had never experienced quite so deeply before. "I can guess," he said grimly.

"Yes, I imagine you can."

"Annie—"

"Don't ever come back to Makawsa," she said in a soft, harsh voice of agonized emotion.

"Annie, you're going to listen to me—"

"You're not welcome here anymore, Mr. Hagen."

"Dammit, *listen!*" he commanded, and she got a sense of the other Matt Hagen in those words. "I *love* you." He sounded desperate and angry.

"That doesn't change much," she croaked out, her

195

voice cracking. "I don't want to lay eyes on you again."

"Annie!"

She hung up on him. She stood by the telephone, almost expecting him to call back immediately. She wiped the tears away fiercely, her throat aching. The telephone remained silent. She knew she should be relieved that he had gotten her message clearly enough the first time, but all she felt was gut-wrenching pain and a hot, hard lump in her chest.

Katie opened her bedroom door. Annie glanced away quickly, trying to wipe away the tears and force her features into a calmer expression.

"Mommy, why're you crying? Isn't Matt coming this weekend?"

"No, honey," she said thickly. "Not this weekend." She wasn't up to explaining that he wasn't coming back at all.

14

KATIE LEFT FOR school as usual the next morning. Annie walked her down to the bus stop, and Katie hugged her tightly. "I hope you feel better, Mommy," she said, gazing up at her. "Don't worry. Matt will come back."

Annie's mouth trembled. "Have a good day at school."

She walked back up the driveway, feeling lonelier than she had in her entire life, even after the divorce from Brent had become final and she was ready to deliver Katie alone in a big city hospital.

The telephone was ringing when Annie came in the front door. She didn't answer it. She was painting pink elephants an hour later when it rang again. Katie would scarcely have begun school, so it had to be Marsha Kintrick or Matt, neither of whom Annie could handle at the moment. The phone rang twenty times before it finally stopped. It rang again five times later.

Annie worked past lunch, her head throbbing. She had hardly slept since Marsha had brought the newspapers Monday morning.

She heard a car in the drive. It was Friday, and she wondered if she could face weekend guests. After untying her apron, she laid it over her stool before going out to see who had arrived.

She stepped into her moccasins, opened the front door, and went outside. Matt was just coming around the front of his blue van, heading for the steps.

"I told you never to come here again! Go *away!*" she cried out, whirling to go back inside the house. She heard him coming and glanced back to see him taking the stairs three at a time. She whipped open the screen door and scrambled inside, trying to slam the front door in his face. But he blocked her, propelling it back as he started to come in. "We're going to talk, Annie," he said in a hard, determined voice, his face pale.

"Get out!"

He looked down at her and frowned darkly. She knew he was seeing the same drawn, pale face with dull, red-rimmed eyes she had seen this morning when she'd brushed her hair in front of the bathroom mirror. "Oh, Annie . . ." he said with regret.

Her eyes welled with tears at his gentle tone, which incensed her all the more. "I told you on the telephone last night that I never wanted to see you again." She pointed toward the door through which he had forced himself.

He closed it behind him. "We're going to talk about all of it."

Her outstretched hand clenched and shook. "No, we are not. I don't want to hear anything you have to say."

"Why not? Because you'll have to make a decision based on fact instead of hearsay and rumors?" he demanded, straightening from the door and taking a step toward her. Her heart leaped sharply, and she retreated into the living room, knowing that if he touched her, she'd be lost. "Don't look at me like that," he said harshly, following her. "I'm not some criminal, Annie."

"No? What about the investigation into kickbacks and your sudden, inexplicable disappearance?" she challenged, standing in the middle of the room, trying to regain some semblance of control. "Here. Look for yourself," she said, turning to the bin next to the fireplace to take out the stack of red-inked newspapers.

She carried them across to the table and slammed them down, flipping pages.

He looked from them to her, his mouth tightening and his eyes narrowing angrily. "Good friend you've got, hmm? Where did she dig all these up?"

"In her trash."

"There was an investigation, yes. I bought a company whose previous owner was involved in government bribes. As a result, I got dragged into the mess he left. I was exonerated completely, cleared unquestionably of any wrong doing. Unfortunately, my innocence didn't make front-page news."

"What about the man you got elected to the board of supervisors?" She yanked out another paper. "This one."

"He was a friend from college days." He let out his breath sharply and rubbed the back of his neck. "I gave him a campaign contribution, yes, but he was duly elected by the public, not me."

"Men like you always have rationalizations and explanations for everything they do, don't they?" she said tightly. "You're just the sort of man I never wanted to love again. Money: That's what you worship. That's your purpose in life, the almighty buck! The more the better, and who cares who you hurt or what you have to do to get it!"

"Part of that was true at one time," he agreed grimly, approaching her, "though I never went beyond the law. I told you that myself the first weekend I stayed here, Annie. It's why I left the city in the first place and traveled for sixteen months—because the almighty buck had come to mean too much."

"You didn't travel. You *escaped!*"

"You're just so damn afraid to trust yourself about me that you're trying to throw us away. You're hiding from it—"

"Just get out of here," she interrupted in a low, hoarse whisper, pointing at the door again.

"My grandfather came to this country from Norway," he said doggedly, "and worked as a common laborer because he couldn't get work as a draftsman. My father spent his life making other men rich on his work and wits. Well, I wanted to make it for myself," he told her, his eyes glittering.

"And you did."

"Yes, I did." He wasn't ashamed of it.

"With seaside condominiums that ruin the view of the beach, by helping elect your friends to public office so you can have favors, by buying and selling companies that involve hundreds of people's lives."

"You're letting those damn newspapers brainwash you. Half of what they printed is speculation and innuendo, and you're quoting it like gospel. The seaside condos didn't go through, as it happens. I invested elsewhere. As for the rest, I'm doing what I can to—"

"Wheel and deal some more? That's what all those calls from Jerry Whoever were about, weren't they? And that slimy man in his ritzy foreign sports car! He's one of your friends from the good old days, too."

"I wouldn't sell Crandall my old used socks," he retorted. "You heard me say as much to him on the telephone a few weeks ago. And Jerry's company has been managing my business interests during my absence."

"Lucrative for him, I'm sure."

Matt's mouth tightened, and his eyes darkened. "As a matter of fact, yes. Which is why he's been trying his best to talk me into hanging on instead of selling out."

"I thought you'd already sold out," she said insultingly, repeating the same cutting words she'd once flung at Brent. They had finally broken the last slender thread that had held them together—because she had wanted it broken.

Matt went very still. "Now you're trying to make me mad," he said very softly, his body rigid. "I was a high roller, granted. I don't deny that. But I earned everything I ever made by *honest effort.* If you want to check that out, you can go through the court records of that investigation." He stepped still closer. "The only major difference between us, Annie, is the scale of business we deal in. I work fourteen hours a day in an office twenty floors up, and you do the same in your workroom. Either way, we both work for a living. One of those necessary evils in the real world you'd like to run away from but can't."

"I'm not the one who ran away."

"Nor am I."

"You don't even look the same! You come up here looking . . . like one of us. But in the city, you put on your real values along with your three-piece business suit."

"And you go to Santa Rosa in a silk dress with your hair up. I don't meet clients dressed in jeans any more than you would meet yours wearing moccasins and a long skirt."

Her eyes burned. "Don't you dare try to put me in your world. My ex-husband was an expert at twisting my head around to make me feel juvenile and unrealistic about the way the world is. He started out to be a public defender, all for the underdog, and ended up finding legal loopholes for the wealthy! Maybe that's the way things are in the *real world*, but that's not a world I want for me or my daughter." She moved back a step, wanting to put distance between them. "And here you are, the big success he clawed for, trying to do a grand whitewash."

His face was pale and taut with anger. "I'm not trying to whitewash anything, Annie. I'm not the same man now that I was a few years ago."

"And what brought about this miraculous change of character? A good scare from the Justice Department?"

"No, a call from a friend who needed to talk. I was too busy making the latest deal for a lot of money, and I put him off. I found out the next day he'd shot himself to death."

Annie felt the blood drain out of her face. She put a trembling hand to her lips, her eyes filling with sudden tears. The raw look in Matt's eyes hurt unbearably.

"Maybe a few drinks and conversation wouldn't have altered things," he went on huskily, "but what I was doing wasn't as important as spending a few minutes with a friend who needed to talk." He pushed his hands into his pockets and continued more quietly. "That's when I began to ask myself what I was doing and why." He regarded her steadily, hiding nothing. "Not everyone is like you, Annie, knowing from the beginning what's most important in this world . . . caring about people. Some of us have to go through an ordeal of discovery first. Sometimes it hurts like hell to take a good look at yourself."

Her throat ached at the pain she saw in his face. She wanted to say it was all right, that she understood, but she couldn't.

"You feel guilty," she managed to say at last, feeling for him, and hurting too.

"Yes. I still do to a certain extent," he admitted softly, understanding the point she was making. "But that wasn't the basis of my decision to get away from things for a while and reevaluate my priorities. I'd always felt somehow discontented. I'd never asked why. I'd thought I just needed more of everything, but it never satisfied whatever it was that ate at me. Jack's death was the catalyst that made me really look at the way I was living and where I was going. And for what."

"But you didn't really change anything, did you?" she said simply.

Matt frowned, his eyes searching hers. "I did

change things, Annie. I walked away from it for six-teen months."

"Not really," she said, her eyes blurring. "You left your old life for a while, yes, but you turned every-thing over to your management experts to keep it going until you came back. And you're back again now, aren't you? You said just the other day that you were putting together the biggest deal of your life." She drew in a ragged breath. "You've been caught between worlds for a while, just as you said yourself. Two days at Makawsa with us to fourteen in your high-city office with your wheeling and dealing. Not a good ratio even if you'd meant it."

"Annie, it's not that simple. A lot of people depend on me. I can't just dump things helter-skelter, or sell out to someone like Crandall. I want to get clear in good conscience and at a fair price."

"There's always a reason for everything people do, right or wrong. I don't want to hear your excuses," she said with quiet finality.

He looked at her for a long moment, his face pale, his eyes bleak, a faint anger burning behind it all. "It's not just what you read, is it, Annie? You just don't have enough faith in your own instincts about people. I've been straight with you, Annie, all the way. And you fell in love with me. Not as fast as I fell in love with you, maybe, but in love nonetheless. That scared you to death. You kept waiting for the disillusionment to come. You think that because you made one mistake, you're making another one." He stepped toward her. "Annie . . ."

She drew back, shaking inside with an old, deep grief.

Matt stood where he was for a long moment, looking down at her in pained silence. "When are you going to put away those old hurts?"

She tried to wipe all the expression off her face, physically aching inside from emotional anguish.

Matt watched. "You put up your walls and withdraw your bridge, Annie, but if you ever get lonely in your tower, remember I'm only a phone call away." He pulled out his wallet, took out a business card, and held it out to her. She wrapped her arms around herself, refusing to take it. He tossed it onto the pile of newspapers strewn across her coffee table. When he looked at her again, she saw the bright sheen of moisture in his blue eyes. "I love you. You think about that," he said, and walked toward the front door.

Katie came in just as he reached it. She looked up at him with a bright smile that fell almost immediately. "What's the matter?" She looked past him to Annie, who was standing pale and rigid in the living room. "What's the matter?" she repeated.

"Matt's leaving, honey," Annie said, the muscles in her face aching from holding back the hot tears that were congealing in her throat and chest.

"But you'll come back again," Katie said, looking up at him with wide, frightened eyes, sensing that something was very wrong.

Matt touched her cheek for a brief moment, looking

down at her, then lightly tugged her pigtail. "Sorry, Kitten." He went out, closing the door behind him.

Annie put her hand over her mouth and tried not to recognize the look in Katie's eyes: hope smashed.

"Mommy, tell him to stay," Katie pleaded, opening the door again. Annie heard the door of the van slam. "Matt, wait!" Katie cried. She turned desperately back to Annie. "Mommy!"

Annie could hear the gravel crunch as Matt backed the van around, the grinding of gears, and then the van moving forward again. Her heart pounded in sickening jolts. She lowered her hand as silence filled the room, feeling faintly nauseated by the grip of so many powerful emotions.

Squatting down, she held her arms out. "Katie, come here, honey. I have to explain—"

"Why is he leaving?" Katie cried, her eyes filled with tears, her mouth trembling.

"Because I asked him to," Annie said, lowering her arms slowly, knowing she couldn't avoid telling her now.

Katie stared at her. "But . . . but he *loves* us."

"Katie—"

"He *does!*"

"You don't understand, honey," she said, the age-old remark of the adult who doesn't really have an answer to give to the child.

"I *do* understand," Katie said bitterly, tears spilling down her pale cheeks, her eyes ablaze with fierce anger. "You did the same thing to my daddy."

Annie's eyes widened. "Katie, I did not!" She stood up shakily, stunned by the unfair accusation. "You don't know anything about that."

"You made him go away, too, didn't you? Didn't you! I know you did, just like you made Matt go away now. You divorced my daddy. I'll bet Daddy *wants* me to come stay with him in the summer and you say no. I'll bet he writes me letters and you throw them all away. He doesn't ever come here to see me because *you're* here! He doesn't hate *me!*"

"Katie, he doesn't hate either one of us," Annie said in a soothing tone, approaching her daughter with her arms out, wanting to comfort her, seeing the long built-up hurts and misconceptions that Brent's neglect had caused. The truth was, Brent just didn't care at all.

"He hates *you!*" Katie screamed at her hysterically. "And I hate you too! I hate you! *I hate you!*"

"Katie!" Annie cried, stricken. Katie plunged out the door and raced down the steps. "Katie!" she called, running after her, alarmed. She saw she was heading down the gravel driveway in the direction Matt had gone. She was out of sight by the time Annie reached the bend in the road.

"Katie!" she cried, sobbing.

15

ANNIE SPENT THREE distraught hours searching frantically for Katie. She ran down the driveway and inland along the winding country road, sure Katie had set out to follow Matt. When she couldn't find her, she went back for the car and looked again. She drove four miles and then backtracked, looking from one side of the road to the other, calling Katie's name periodically, seeing nothing.

Where was she?

It was nearing dusk, and Annie still hadn't found her.

She called Marsha, hoping Katie had gone in the other direction and run away to her friend's house three miles down the road. "No, Annie, she's not here. Listen, don't worry about it. She'll come home before dark."

"What if she doesn't?"

"Then we'll get some people together and go out and find her," Marsha said. "Kids do these things. Suzanne ran away a month ago because we wouldn't take her on the Skunk Train. Ted found her sulking in her tree house."

But Katie's reasons for running away went far deeper than pique over a train ride.

Annie went down to the river where Katie and Matt

had skipped stones. "Katie!" she called, walking all along the wooded trail up to the meadow above the farmhouse. "Katie!" She raced down the hill by the fern trail, scrambling over the fallen redwood and running on again until she reached the barn. "Katie?" She climbed up to the loft Matt had built. Katie wasn't there. "Please, God, let me find her . . ." She went to the chicken house, the carport, down the hill again to the swing and tool shed. She went into the house and checked Katie's room.

It was almost dark outside.

In desperation, she went to the coffee table and picked up Matt's card. Her hand was shaking so badly she almost couldn't dial the number. It rang once, twice, three times.

"Oh, please . . ." she whispered brokenly, her eyes tightly closed.

"Hello."

She felt a wave of intense relief at the sound of his voice. "M—Matt . . ."

"Annie?"

"Oh, Matt," she cried, "Katie's gone. She ran away right after you left. I've looked *everywhere*."

"I'm on my way."

How many hours would it take him to get there? Three? Four? It was so dark outside. Where was Katie?

She called Marsha again. "Marsha, have Ted get some people together, please. She's not back."

"We'll start right now. You stay next to the telephone." Marsha called back a few minutes later to tell Annie that a couple of men were driving north and south of Gualala to see if Katie might have gone that way. Mr. Roskowick was with them. "They've all got CB's, so we'll hear the minute they find her. If she comes home, call me right away, and I'll let them know. All right? Annie, she'll be okay." But in an hour Katie still wasn't home.

Annie sat down on the front steps, looking into the darkness around the house and the barn and the chicken house, her front door open so she could hear the telephone if it rang.

She heard a helicopter in the distance. It came closer, and the air-whomping whirl grew louder until the machine hovered right over her driveway and slowly settled to the ground in front of the house. The frightening *whosh-whosh* of the huge rotor blades slowed as the engine whined down. She thought it must be the police, but it was Matt who appeared from the clear fiberglass dome. Annie stood up and came down the steps, trembling.

"Has she come back yet?" he demanded.

She shook her head, her eyes blurring again, her mouth quivering.

"I think I might know where she is," he told her, coming close, his face grim as he saw the ravages of her worry. "Go on inside, Annie."

He was gone for half an hour. The telephone rang. Annie answered quickly. It was Marsha. "Anything yet?" she asked Annie hopefully.

"No." Annie's heart sank. The screen door opened behind her, and she glanced back quickly. "Yes! She's here. *She's here,* Marsha!"

"Thank *God.* I'll let the men know."

Annie's heart constricted as she looked at Katie's tear-stained, dirty face and bedraggled appearance.

"She's all right, Annie," Matt said, standing behind Katie, his hands on her thin shoulders. Katie catapulted forward into Annie's arms, hugging her fiercely.

"I'm sorry, Mommy. I didn't mean it," she said between sobs and hiccups.

"I know. It's all right," Annie choked out, clasping her as close as she could without crushing her. She drew back finally and tipped up Katie's quivering chin. "You need a bath, young lady," she said.

Katie looked back over her shoulder at Matt, who was still standing in the doorway. "I'm not leaving, Kitten," he assured her gently, winking at her.

Annie's heart squeezed tight.

Katie was almost asleep on her feet by the time Annie had bathed her and was helping to dress her in her woolly Strawberry Shortcake pajamas. Annie lifted her, and Katie wrapped her arms around her neck and her legs around her waist, resting her head on her shoulder. "I want Matt to tuck me in, Mommy," she murmured.

Annie felt a shock at the request. "All right, honey," she said shakily. She carried her out into the hallway. "Matt?" He came out of the living room.

Katie lifted her head and looked at him. She let go of Annie with one hand to reach out for him. Annie bit down on her lower lip and avoided his eyes as she let him take Katie. She stood in the bedroom doorway as he carried her to bed. Katie caught hold of him, saying something. He sat down on the side of her bed and brushed her hair back gently from her temples and talked to her softly.

Annie turned away. She went into the kitchen and sat down, putting her head in her arms. Matt found her that way a few minutes later. He put his hand gently on her shoulder and squeezed lightly. "She'll be fine."

"Will she?" she muttered thickly, raising her head to look at him bleakly. "I haven't even thanked you. I don't know what I would have done, Matt."

"I love her, too, Annie," he whispered hoarsely. "This isn't easy on any of us."

"I know you love her." She watched him walk across to the cabinet and take down the can of coffee.

"Do you mind?" he asked, and she shook her head.

"Where was she, Matt?"

He filled the pot with water. "In her special hideout," he said, glancing at her with a frown and beginning to measure coffee into the filter basket.

"I thought I knew all her special places," Annie murmured, deeply hurt.

"You do. Except this one, which was a secret she kept to herself."

"But shared with you."

"Annie . . ."

"I know," she said wearily. "Only . . ." She looked up at him. "It hurts," she whispered. "I feel as if I've lost her."

"You haven't." He came back and sat down at the table with her. She started to cry again. "Annie, don't . . ."

"She's got things all muddled up in her little head, Matt. She doesn't know anything about the divorce. All she knows is that her father never comes, never calls, never writes. She thinks he sends her Christmas and birthday presents, but he doesn't. I buy those things and wrap them up for her and put his name on them because I can't bear for her to go through what I did." Her voice cracked, and she looked away, trying to force down the old hurt. She sat for a minute, fighting another bout of tears. Matt sat waiting silently.

"I can't tell her the truth, Matt," she told him softly. "Brent doesn't love her. You asked me once about the straw that broke this camel's back. It was . . . it was when he asked me to abort my pregnancy. To abort Katie."

Matt's face darkened.

"Brent said there wasn't enough money for a baby. He had just been offered a junior partnership in a big New York law firm. No money for a baby, he said, because we'd have to fix up an apartment for entertaining clients." She closed her eyes, cringing inwardly. "How could I ever have loved someone so shallow? But I did," she said huskily. "In the begin-

213

ning, when I met him, he was . . . he was full of ideals. He used to give speeches in front of Sproul Hall, protesting Vietnam and third world starvation and nuclear armament." She sighed heavily and looked across the table. She made an attempt at a smile. "Just words." Her mouth trembled. "You were probably working on your business degree and making plans for your future success."

His expression was enigmatic. "No. I never gave any speeches, Annie. I enlisted in the Marine Corps and went to Vietnam. When I came back, I went through college on the GI bill. After that, I worked in real estate until I had the money to go into my own business." He was giving her information without reprimand.

She looked at him and wanted to cry all over again, this time for different reasons. "Is that where you learned to fly that helicopter?"

His eyes softened at her tone. "No. I learned back here in the States. Jack, the man who killed himself, was the pilot in Nam. I was his door gunner."

She just looked at him, knowing she loved him more than she ever had any other man. "So you must have saved his life a few times, too, Matt."

He rested his arms on the kitchen table, leaning toward her. "Tell me the rest, Annie. What happened with your father?"

She winced. "He left my mother when I was Katie's age. At first I thought it was my fault; then I blamed my mother. Just as Katie's blaming me. It was a long time before I fully understood that he just didn't want the responsibility of marriage and children, or a steady job. My mother always loved him. All I knew was that I wanted my father to come home, and he never did."

The warmth in Matt Hagen's eyes was soothing balm for the old wounds.

"Oh, Matt, I'm sorry I ever said you were like either one of them," she whispered brokenly. "You're not. You've been here every time I needed you. I know that . . . only . . ."

He reached out and took her hand. "I know, Annie." He stroked her palm with his thumb. "You've got to get some rest," he told her softly.

"I can't live in your world, Matt," she told him, "and you don't really belong in mine."

His hand tightened. "We'll talk about all that in the morning." He let go of her.

After a moment she got up. Just before she went out the door, she said, "I wish there were no such thing as a newspaper."

"No, I should have told you what I was trying to do from the beginning, instead of letting it wait."

16

ANNIE DREAMED MATT was kissing her. Slow kisses traveled up the soft skin of her throat, then over her ear and temple, her cheek, across to the other temple. She rolled over slowly onto her back, gave a soft, shaky sigh, and felt his warm, firm mouth cover hers. Her heart thumped faster as she felt his hand, big and strong, cup her breast for a moment and then glide down to her hip.

"Wake up, sleepyhead," he whispered against her throat, and she smelled the damp cleanliness of his hair. She reached up lazily and touched the rough stubble of his day-old beard. He rubbed his mouth sinuously against the sensitive skin in the hollow above her collarbone, and she arched her back. "Hmm, Annie, you're warmer than toast . . ."

She opened her eyes. He was really here, sitting on the edge of her bed. He leaned back slightly and brushed the hair back from her cheeks. He smiled at her.

"What time is it?" she asked, feeling oddly close to tears again even though she'd thought she had cried everything out last night before going to sleep.

"Ten."

"Oh! Katie missed her bus," she said, starting to push herself up.

"Everything's well in hand, Annie," Matt told her, so confident that she relaxed.

"I thought I set it for six."

"I shut it off. You were worn out," he told her. "You needed a good night's sleep. I don't think you've had one since your friend foisted all those old newspapers on you."

Her eyes filled again at the mention of them. She noticed that Matt looked tired, too. Lines were deeply etched about his blue eyes, and he looked grim. He needed a shave. She could still feel where his beard had rubbed her.

"I love you, Annie."

"I know. I love you, too."

He reached over to her bedside table and picked up a tray. She had thought she was imagining the smell of bacon and coffee, but saw that he had brought her breakfast. She looked up at him. "Thank you."

"Anything for my lady."

"Oh, Matt . . ." She just couldn't cry anymore, could she?

He stood up and looked down at her. "When you're finished, pack a few things for yourself and Katie. I'm taking you both back to the city with me this morning." He ran his index finger down along the line of her cheek. "Annie, showing you what I've been having to deal with is much simpler than trying to explain anything."

She watched him walk to the door. "Matt . . ."

"Don't argue, Annie," he said, not looking back, his

shoulders squared.

"I wasn't going to," she said softly. "If you want a shave, my safety razor is in the medicine cabinet. The new blades are right beside it."

He looked back at her, his gaze warm. Then he went out.

Annie held Katie securely on her lap as the whine of the engine and the *whosh* of the helicopter blades began. She could feel the odd vibrations running through her body like static electricity on a dry, wintry day. Katie laughed, full of excitement at this new experience.

"Hold still, honey."

Annie glanced at Matt, who looked so unfamiliar in his radio headset, his hands working the controls. He glanced at her. "Scared?" She couldn't hear the word because of the deafening noise, but she understood him by the way he mouthed the word carefully. She forced a smile and shook her head, but as a weightless sensation assailed her and the helicopter rose, her heart ascended into her throat. Matt smiled at her. "It's okay," he mouthed.

"Mommy! Look at the trees! We're higher than the trees!" Katie cried out.

Annie saw the farmhouse below and the grass and flowers laid back flat in a wide circle, rippling with the pulse of the whirling blades taking them up. She swallowed convulsively. The front of the helicopter dipped slightly and the vehicle surged forward. Annie clutched tightly at Katie and pulled her firmly against her.

Annie thought she would get used to the experience, but her fear was still strong as they neared the city. She could feel the wind every time it buffeted the vulnerable chopper, sending it forward with a surge of heightened speed or in a heavy sideways lift for a few seconds.

Below lay gray-blue, white-capped waves. As they raced across the bay and the towering buildings of San Francisco came up, she could see the Transamerica Pyramid pointing heavenward.

"There's Fisherman's Wharf!" Katie cried, and Annie felt her wiggling forward and clutched her even tighter. "Oh, Matt, can we fly over the aquarium?"

Annie prayed fervently that he wouldn't, that he would just land this contraption. A moment later she felt the sensation of hovering. She opened her eyes and looked around. They were still high up and smack-dab in the middle of the city. She chanced a look down and saw car-jammed streets. Matt was setting them down on top of a building. Below them was a great circle painted on a square roof. A man on the roof was giving them signals, wind from the rotors rippling his jacket and blowing his hair wildly. Then the helicopter touched down, and the rotors chop-chopped more slowly as the engine slowly died.

Annie breathed easily again.

Matt took off his headset and leaned toward her, his hand curving warmly against her neck and drawing her toward him so he could say in her ear, "Sorry that was such an ordeal. We'll drive home."

The man who had been signaling opened her door and lifted Katie out. Although the rotors were well above her head, Annie ducked instinctively as she uncurled from her seat and got out. She caught hold of Katie's hand and pulled her closer.

Matt came around and put his warm, firm hand around her waist, drawing her toward the small entryway in the corner. "We'll go down over there," he told her.

Once inside, the chill air of San Francisco was shut out and warmth relaxed Annie even more. Near the door, a man in a gray business suit was sitting at a big desk. He raised a hand to Matt in greeting and smiled in warm welcome as Matt introduced them. From there they went into the hallway, and Matt punched the button for an elevator. "This is my main office building," he explained.

"Impressive," was all she could say.

"I own three buildings," he told her. "This one, another out in Burlingame near the airport, and the other across in Oakland a few blocks from Jack London Square."

She didn't say anything else as they entered the elevator, but there was a sick feeling in the pit of her stomach. She could feel Matt watching her as the elevator went down. Katie was standing between them, one hand in Annie's and the other in Matt's. She was watching the floor register lighting up numbers. "Oh, this is fun! Can we do it again?"

Matt laughed softly. When they arrived at the first floor, he reached over and punched the button for the top floor. Katie giggled. "Oh, it makes my tummy feel funny."

All Annie could think of were twenty floors of office building, and this was only one that he owned.

"You can ride in Warren's elevator while your mom and I talk in my office. When you get tired of it, he'll show you where we are."

Once Warren had his instructions and Katie was sent on her adventurous yo-yo ride with the elevator attendant, Matt ushered Annie to his offices on the eighteenth floor.

A middle-aged, friendly-faced woman dressed elegantly in a fitted, rust-colored business suit and a cream silk blouse sat at a desk in front of his office door. She greeted him warmly, and he introduced Annie again before opening the door. Annie sensed Mrs. Cierzan's sincere warmth and friendly interest. "So this is the young lady," she said smiling.

When Matt took Annie into his office, she looked around at the paneled walls and the great windows offering a panoramic view of San Francisco in the direction of Twin Peaks. Matt's mahogany desk was big enough to fill her entire workroom. The comfortable chairs and couch were covered in soft leather. The three ficus trees near the windows were three times the size of her own and didn't overwhelm the large office at all. In fact, the big bedroom and living room of Makawsa could have fit easily into this massive office suite.

"May I sit down?" she asked softly, and did so before her knees gave way completely. She was shaking. She looked up at Matt as he leaned back against his desk, stretching out one hard-muscled, jean-clad leg while he dangled the other. Leaning forward slightly, he clasped his hands loosely.

"You look like someone just punched you hard in the stomach, Annie," he murmured grimly.

"It's an apt description of the way I feel," she murmured, swallowing heavily as she looked around again. Matt Hagen had reached the epitome of what Brent had only dreamed of attaining. "Just three buildings?" she tried to joke. It fell flat.

"I owned an apartment complex in Danville, but I sold that almost a month ago. It's cleared escrow."

"Oh." She clenched her hands together in her lap. "How . . . how many ventures have you been involved in, Matt?"

"Why don't we start at the beginning so you won't get things by halves?" he suggested, straightening. She watched him walk across to the elegant bookcases against the wall, open a cabinet, and pour something into a snifter. He carried it back and handed it to her.

"It's barely noon," she protested.

"Your face is the color of paste," he told her. He bent and put his hand over hers. "And you're cold as ice. Here."

"All right." She sipped tentatively, then looked up at him, trying to prepare herself.

He leaned back against the desk again, remaining close to her. "I started by selling real estate for a construction company in the southeast Bay Area during the big boom in building about twelve years ago. I made a lot of money in a short time and had to invest it," he explained. "So I invested some in a new shopping center being built in San Jose and the rest in an apartment complex in Hayward. I sold out of those ventures and put my profits into two office buildings, the one in Burlingame and the other in Oakland. When the seaside condos came along, I had money to invest again and did so. But that didn't work out, as you already know, and I went into partnership to buy this building. With Crandall."

"Oh."

Matt sighed. "The deal I was negotiating when my marine friend Jack called was the one that bought out Crandall's share. He was having financial trouble, and I wanted him out. So I extended myself as far as I could and took over the building completely."

"And he wants back in again?" she said.

"I sent word to Jerry about six months ago that I wanted to sell all my holdings, this building included. Crandall was the first to make an offer, which I rejected."

"Why?"

"Because he'd raise costs so high that some of the companies who lease space in the buildings would go under. And that would put people out of work. Luckily another offer has come in. The price is about the same, but this fellow, Carstairs, has a better reputation. I've dealt with him before."

Mrs. Cierzan opened the door before he could continue, and Annie looked away. "There's a pretty young lady looking for you two." The secretary smiled and escorted Katie in before closing the door again.

"Warren told me some funny jokes, Mommy," she said, skipping across the plush cream carpet. "What kind of pet does a barber like? A *hare!* Isn't that funny?" She laughed, her eyes sparkling. She was high with everything—the helicopter ride, the city, going up and down in the elevator. "Wait till I tell Suzanne!"

"Hold up, Katie," Matt said, catching her beneath the arms and lifting her onto his hard thigh. "Give your mom a chance to breathe. How would you like a tour of the city? We'll all go to the aquarium for a few hours, have a snack at the Japanese Gardens, then go down to Fisherman's Wharf for dinner."

"Oh, *can* we?"

"Wouldn't've suggested it if we couldn't." He grinned, and looked at Annie sitting silently in the chair. "What do you say, Annie?" he asked softly.

"Yes," she agreed, just wanting to get out of this building.

Annie walked slowly behind Katie along the myriad darkened corridors of the aquarium and looked into the lighted netherworld of tanks filled with exotic and sometimes colorful undersea creatures. She read the identifications as Katie pressed forward to peer through the huge glass walls, wide-eyed at the wonder of it all.

Matt was right behind her. He had taken Annie's hand once, but she had withdrawn it, tucking both hands protectively into the pockets of her dark navy pea-coat. He didn't try to touch her again or break her silence. She tried to analyze her own confused emotions.

Money changed people. It had changed Brent. Now, here was Matt saying that none of it mattered. He was "getting rid of a few things he didn't need."

When they went into the Museum of Natural History, Annie sat on a bench in a big room while Matt took Katie around to each of the displays of stuffed animals in their natural habitats. Annie watched them together and recognized that Matt really loved Katie, and that the bond between them had grown as close as that between a natural father and his child. She ached watching them.

She loved him so much, but more than seven years ago she had rejected the same world in which she now found that Matt thrived. Where Brent had yearned to go, Matt had gone successfully. She believed he had done it through hard work. But so much went along with it. All those cocktail parties full of strangers, and looking right and playing a part for the sake of impressing clients. She hated all that.

She belonged to Makawsa.

When Matt walked toward her, Katie holding his

hand, Annie couldn't look up at him, knowing that if she did, she would start crying all over again. Katie was too excited about what she was seeing to notice anything wrong. But Matt did.

They went to the Japanese Tea Gardens, and Annie took Katie along the winding, beautifully landscaped paths and the bonsai trees and flowering shrubs. Katie raced to the top of every arched bridge to lean over and watch the fat golden carp weave through the murky water. Glittering copper pennies that wish-makers had cast in sparkled on the bottom.

When they rejoined Matt, he ordered Katie a chocolate milkshake and a small basket of fortune cookies. Annie had tea. He watched her steadily, even while managing to field Katie's hundred questions.

Annie avoided his intent gaze and reached for a fortune cookie, crumbling it with trembling fingers. "What's it say, Mommy?"

Annie raised her eyes briefly to meet Matt's and then crumpled the paper quickly, dropping it into the empty ashtray. "Just nonsense," she said, shaking her head.

"What'd it say?" Katie persisted. Matt reached out for it.

"Just leave it, please," Annie said.

"That bad?" he asked with a wry smile. Then, to divert Katie from further questions, he said, "What do you say we head down to the wharf?"

They walked back across toward the museum parking lot, Katie hopping along just in front of them, all energy and joyous excitement. Matt caught Annie's hand. She tried to draw it away, but he wove his fingers firmly between hers.

"You're not getting away from me that easily," he said huskily, and she knew he didn't mean just for the day. She felt the strength and warmth of his large hand.

Katie reached the van. Matt unlocked the side door for her and slid it back so she could jump in. He turned to Annie, still holding her hand tightly. He raised the other hand, sliding it beneath her braid and clasping it around her neck to draw her forward.

"Don't, Matt," she murmured brokenly.

His eyes searched hers bleakly. "Annie, stop trying to think of a way to end it between us and instead help us find a way to make it work. I'm getting out."

She wanted to cry at the expression on his face. "How can you? You're in so deep."

"You're copping out, dammit!"

She flinched. "This isn't the time to discuss it," she pleaded.

He let go long enough to slide the door closed with a bang, blocking Katie's view, and then yanked Annie against him, crushing her mouth under his. She gasped at the onslaught, and the slow chill that had held her body in such a tight grip for days melted in a rush of heat and life.

Someone gave a shrill wolf whistle nearby. Matt drew back, his eyes dark and brooding. "You're right. We can't talk here."

They drove to the wharf and took Katie to the old sailing ship *Balclutha*, which was permanently docked there and open to tourists. Matt kept reminding Annie how he could make her feel. When the wind blew her braid across her breasts, he gently brushed it back, sending her pulse reeling. As she peered into a ship's cabin, he came up behind her and put his hands on her hips as he looked over her shoulder into the small cubbyhole. She caught her breath as she felt his fingers spread against her abdomen, and again as he brushed a light kiss against the curve of her neck.

Katie stayed close, both frightened and excited by the huge milling crowds along the open-air corridor outside Alioto's Number Eight. Inside, Matt spoke to the maître d', and within a few minutes they were seated at a premium table next to the windows overlooking the fishing fleet.

It was another reminder of who he really was, she thought, glancing at him. One murmured word to a maître d', and a weekend crowd of hungry tourists was parted like the Red Sea so that Matt Hagen could be seated.

"Other people were waiting ahead of us," she told him.

"I made reservations before we left Makawsa."

"Oh." She felt ashamed.

"Can I have a hamburger?" Katie asked, looking from one to the other.

Matt laughed softly. "No, you can't. You're going to have lobster, just the way you've always said you would if you got the chance."

While they had dinner, Katie asked endless questions which Matt answered patiently. He knew a great deal about the city, but Annie found herself watching his face—the way his eyes sparkled as he talked with Katie, how he looked at her.

He *did* love them both.

Katie was winding down by the time she finished a third of her rich meal. "Looks like someone needs a little shuteye," Matt said as Katie snuggled against Annie's side, her eyelids dropping heavily. He signaled the waiter. Annie roused Katie enough to walk her outside.

"Would you carry me, Mommy?" Katie pleaded sleepily, but Matt brushed Annie's hands aside and lifted her.

"She's too heavy for you to carry all the way back to the car," Annie protested, but he ignored her.

They said nothing as they retraced their steps to the van. Katie was sound asleep in spite of the chill wind and the heavy mist coming in from the bay. "The keys are in my front pocket." Matt instructed her.

Annie's heart knocked crazily as she slid her hand into his pocket and felt the hard warmth of his hip. She unlocked the door and stood back after sliding it open so he could duck in and settle Katie securely in back. He slid the door shut, walked around to her side, and then got in.

"Is there a place to stay—"

"We'll be staying at my place," he told her, starting

229

the van and backing it out of the parking space.

"Oh," she said, worried.

He glanced at her briefly. "We still have some things to talk about."

Neither of them spoke as he drove through the crowded city streets. Annie realized within a few minutes that they were winding toward Coit Tower. Matt swung into a short cobblestoned driveway, pressed a button on a small box in his glove compartment, and drove into a two-car garage. A small red Mercedes was already parked inside. Looking at the high sheen of that expensive car, she listened with a thundering heart to the *whir* of the garage door coming down behind them.

"Yours?" she asked, nodding toward the car.

"Yes." He gave her an enigmatic look. "If you'll get the overnight bag, Annie, I'll get Katie. Here's the key to the back door."

Annie followed him through the immaculate, ultra-modern kitchen, then down a hall into a small bedroom. He laid Katie on the single bed. "When you've got her settled, come back the same way but turn left into the living room. We'll talk." His blue eyes held hers compellingly.

Annie dressed Katie in her pajamas and awakened her just enough to explain where they were so she wouldn't be frightened if she woke up in the middle of the night. She tucked her in warmly and kissed her good night.

Matt was standing at the plate-glass windows overlooking San Francisco. The lighted Golden Gate Bridge was visible in the misty distance.

Annie made a quick survey of the living room. It had the gloss of a professional decorator rather than a homey quality. Everything was too exactly in place, too perfectly coordinated in shades of blue, green, and brown.

It was just the sort of place Brent had dreamed of having and probably did have now. The right neighborhood, the right decorator, the right ambience of success and money. It would be perfect for a magazine layout. It told absolutely nothing about the man who lived here.

Annie hated it.

Matt turned and studied her ruefully. He crossed to the white brick fireplace trimmed with elaborately designed tiles and clicked a switch. The fire started, a low romantic glow of golden flame produced by gas jets and licking sinuously against an asbestos log. It looked real—even smelled real with the canned scent of burning pine—but it was fake.

"Not exactly Makawsa," Matt said, nodding in a derisive gesture that took it all in.

"No."

"Three years ago I didn't know the difference. I only felt it," he told her. Their eyes locked across the room. "Annie, you're the first woman I've ever met who's upset because I have money."

"Money is a gross understatement, Matt. You have all the proper status symbols to go along with your position."

"Yes, I noticed how you looked at the Mercedes—like a pile of unspread fertilizer in my garage."

She met his wry expression defensively. "It's none of my business."

His blue eyes ignited. "Nevertheless, you'll condemn, penalize, censure, and convict me without benefit of trial."

"That's not fair," she said shakily. "You were the one who came to Makawsa on false pretenses. I thought you were—"

"A bum. Now you know I'm not. I was never false with you, Annie. You just want to believe that so you can go on with your safe, if lonely, existence in the woods." He came across to her, stopping directly in front of her. "I never lied to you."

"You left out a few things."

"Would you have believed me if I'd claimed to be a millionaire the first day I drove into Makawsa? And why bring it up? I hadn't thought about it for sixteen months. I'd already made some calls to sell off two buildings. I didn't want to come back to this." He let out a deep breath. "I want meaning in my life, Annie. The minute I saw you, I knew you gave me that. You and Katie. But I also knew within a day of being around you that you'd trust me even less as a successful businessman than as someone traveling around for a while." His eyes glittered. "Tell me the truth. Is it the money you so disapprove of, or the fear of what it can do to people?"

"I don't know. With Brent and the people he was

around, money was the ultimate goal."

"With most of the people I knew, too, Annie. But it can also be used to good purpose."

"Is that how you've used yours?" she asked quietly.

"I used my money to make more money," he admitted. "You get to a point in finance where it begins to pyramid. But I worked for everything I ever made, Annie. It wasn't handed to me, and I didn't cheat the public to get it." He sighed heavily, raking a hand back through his thick, dark hair. His expression was grim as he studied her face.

"Annie, you're so convinced I'm just like your ex-husband, like a lot of men and women in business, like much of the world in general. Money as a primary goal, a guideline for how big you are. Business as an end result. Making the right friends and connections, being successful, having all the right accoutrements to go along with it. All that goes along with *making it.* And I did subscribe to all of that." He took her hands. "But, Annie, I started out the way your ex-husband finished. I told you that at Makawsa. I had it all and found it empty. That's when I went looking for something better and found you."

Her eyes softened.

"But you've got to understand something," he told her. "It isn't business itself that's bad. You're in business yourself. It becomes bad when you let it take over your entire life and you lose sight of what's important—being there when someone needs to talk; providing jobs for people; loving someone and making

233

that first in your life. God knows there's more vulnerability in love than in sitting in any boardroom making decisions."

"Are you selling everything, Matt? Was that what you meant before?"

"Not everything, no," he admitted. "The building in Burlingame and the one in Oakland, yes. I'll still retain part interest in the building you saw today." His hands tightened. "Sit down, Annie."

Here it comes, she thought, preparing herself. They sat down on the couch, and he looked at her. "I'm putting most of my money into a new enterprise. All those months I traveled, I was thinking about it. I'm planning to fund a program through the University of California to counsel veterans suffering from delayed stress syndrome."

Her eyes widened. She thought of his friend Jack who'd committed suicide. "Oh, Matt . . ."

"Don't give me any medals, Annie. We've got a long way to go and will need government assistance. But we've made some inroads in the last few weeks. The expertise is there, ready." He touched her cheek and added in total honesty, "I've had to use a few of the old techniques, Annie. Pulling strings, calling on friends I knew in business. Things don't happen just because people care about people."

"It just might take a little longer," she disagreed.

"There are men like Jack who can't wait."

She stood up and walked slowly toward the windows, gazing out at the lights of the city, the glimmering streets, the heavy fog rolling in.

"I . . . I just can't agree with you about everything, Matt."

"If two people agreed on everything all the time, Annie, it would mean one of them wasn't thinking."

She closed her burning eyes.

"Annie, a year and a half ago, I was in the crowd of people you avoided. I led a life you rejected. But I made my own choice, too, Annie. If people can change for the worse, you've got to believe they can change for the better. Rebirth of the spirit—isn't that the belief you subscribe to?" She felt his hands on her shoulders. "I'm still going to be rich," he admitted. "I know you'd rather have fallen in love with a poor man, but you didn't. It's how we deal with it from here on that matters, that we do something worthwhile with our lives."

She leaned back against him, loving him more than she ever had before. "How do we make it work? Won't you have to stay here?"

He turned her around. "We'll find a way," he repeated and kissed her.

She wanted so much to be physically one with him again, that she trembled. She saw the smoldering in his eyes and heard his breath quicken.

"This is real, Annie. I love you. I love Katie. I want to marry you and adopt her. I want us to live at Makawsa."

"But how?" She started to cry, feeling despair.

He cupped his hands around her face. "It won't be

easy. I'm going to have to live between two worlds for a while longer. But I've looked into an advanced computer system. We'd have to make some changes at Makawsa so it could be housed there, but with that, a couple of extensions on your telephone, and my helicopter, it could work."

"Would you be happy there?" she asked worriedly. "It's so different from . . . all this."

"A difference I want. I don't need any of this, Annie. If I did, I wouldn't have left it behind and gone looking for something more all those months ago."

Her heart expanded. He kissed her then, urgently. "Let me convince you," he whispered roughly and lifted her to carry her down the hallway.

"Matt . . ."

He pushed a door open with his shoulder, kicked it shut, and crossed to a big double bed. "Matt . . ." Further words were stifled as he took her mouth, laying her back, coming down with her, his hands already loosening her clothing.

She knew she wanted this as much as he did.

She arched her body to help him free her of the bonds of clothing. He wasn't taking his time as he had in the meadow above the farmhouse. But time wasn't what she needed now. She needed him inside her again, so close that he was part of her.

His hands were strong and unyielding as he lifted her again. He was kneeling, her legs lying across his so that they were facing each other. The look in his blue eyes sent her heart pounding so hard and fast that she felt faint. "I need you always, Annie." He caught her hips firmly and drew her forward, his face taut.

His thighs were hard beneath hers, but she felt him shaking violently. He spread his knees, his hands tightening on her hips, his mouth taking hers as he joined them. He held her that way for a long time, impaled, while he kissed her over and over again. Then he rolled her over, coming down over her and loving her inexorably until she cried out softly and clung to him.

After a moment he turned over again so she was on top of him. He kissed her again. She lay with her head against his chest. "It feels so right," she murmured.

"That's because it is."

Annie heard Katie call out. "Oh, dear," she said, and moved away from Matt. He rolled in the opposite direction and yanked open a dresser drawer. "Here, Annie," he said, tossing her the tops to a set of cotton pajamas. She pulled them on, laughing slightly as she watched him pull on the bottoms.

"Just a minute, honey," she called to Katie. Matt barely managed to get the bottoms up and snapped before Katie opened the bedroom door and walked in. She stood there, rubbing her eyes.

"Everything is fine, honey," Annie said.

Katie looked at her bare legs and Matt's bare chest. "Does this mean you're going to marry Matt and he's going to be my daddy?"

There was nothing like a child to put things in proper perspective. Annie glanced at Matt standing on the other side of the bed. "Yes," she said, smiling.

Matt shoved the covers back and got into bed, gazing up at Annie with amusement and challenge in his eyes as he pulled back the covers on the other side for her to get in. She slid in beside him and beckoned to Katie. She ran to them. Matt, Annie, and Katie pressed together like warm toast in the big bed. They were a family.

"You can't stay all night, honey," Annie whispered after a little while, kissing her daughter's cheek.

"Hmm, I know," Katie murmured sleepily. She wiggled down under the blankets, pressing herself back into Annie's abdomen, curled in the fetal position in which Annie had carried her for nine long, lonely months.

Matt fitted his hard, big body tightly behind Annie and kissed the curve of her neck. He reached across her shoulder and brushed a few strands of hair back from Katie's temple. "First thing you're going to have to learn, Kitten, is to knock before coming into our bedroom."

Katie murmured agreement. She was already half asleep, but she managed to mumble, "When can I have a baby sister?"

Annie felt Matt shaking with soft laughter behind her, and his lips brushed her ear. "A project we can pleasurably collaborate on, hmm?" He bit her ear lightly. "In case I neglected to tell you, I want lots of children."

A few minutes later Matt got up and carried Katie

back to her own bed in the guest room. He returned and slid into bed with Annie, pulling her close and rolling her on top of him and then underneath him. He kissed her deeply for a long time. "Oh, lady," he said finally, "you do fill up all my senses . . ."

He pushed up the pajama top she was wearing and rubbed his hard, furred chest against her full, throbbing breasts while nibbling the sensitive skin along her collarbone. "By the way, what did the fortune in your cookie say?"

"Hmm?" She was thinking that whatever problems came—and problems would aplenty—she knew they would work them out together.

"Your fortune cookie," he repeated.

She combed her hands lovingly through his thick hair and lifted his head to kiss him. "It said: *Your lover will never wish to leave you.*"

"The Chinese are very wise," he said, nuzzling her.

She pressed her mouth against his and kissed him with everything she had bottled up inside for so long, just needing the right man to bring all the love she had to give out of hiding.

"Ohhh, yes," Matt murmured hoarsely after a long time, "my princess has finally torn down her tower."

Center Point Publishing
600 Brooks Road ● PO Box 1
Thorndike ME 04986-0001 USA

(207) 568-3717

US & Canada:
1 800 929-9108